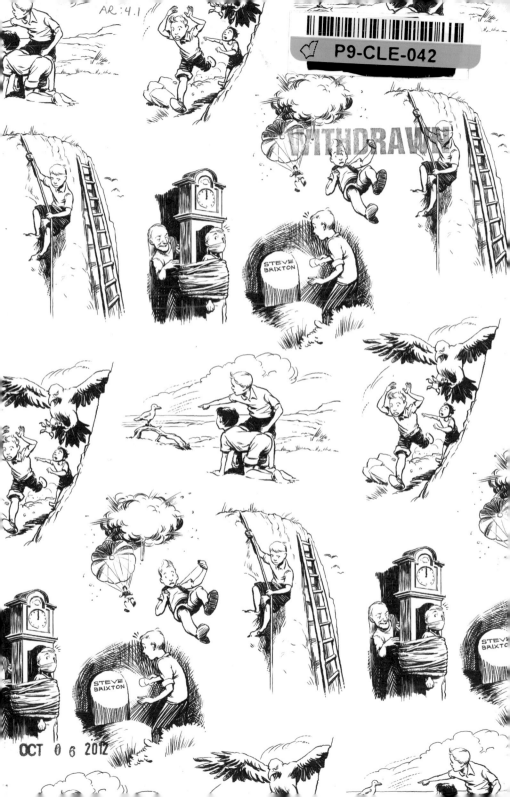

DANGER GOES BERSERK

The Orcas Island Library

Purchased with funds
donated from the

Read all the Brixton Brothers Mysteries:

#1 The Case of the Case of Mistaken Identity

#2 The Ghostwriter Secret

#3 It Happened on a Train

BRIXTON BROTHERS

DANGER GOES BERSERK

BY
Mac Barnett

ILLUSTRATIONS BY
Matthew Myers

SIMON & SCHUSTER BOOKS FOR YOUNG READERS
New York • London • Toronto • Sydney • New Delhi

SIMON & SCHUSTER BOOKS FOR YOUNG READERS
An imprint of Simon & Schuster Children's Publishing Division
1230 Avenue of the Americas, New York, New York 10020

SIMON & SCHUSTER BOOKS FOR YOUNG READERS is a trademark of Simon & Schuster, Inc.
For information about special discounts for bulk purchases, please contact Simon & Schuster Special Sales at 1-866-506-1949 or business@simonandschuster.com.
The Simon & Schuster Speakers Bureau can bring authors to your live event. For more information or to book an event, contact the Simon & Schuster Speakers Bureau at 1-866-248-3049 or visit our website at www.simonspeakers.com.
Book design by Lizzy Bromley
The text for this book is set in Souvenir.
The illustrations for this book are rendered in pencil and digitally.
Manufactured in the United States of America
0812 FFG
2 4 6 8 10 9 7 5 3 1

Library of Congress Cataloging-in-Publication Data
Barnett, Mac.
Danger goes berserk / Mac Barnett ; illustrated by Matthew Myers. — 1st ed.
p. cm. — (Brixton Brothers ; [#4])
Summary: As soon as twelve-year-old Steve Brixton opens a detective office in his backyard, he and his best friend Dana are caught up in a tangle of cases, from breaking up a ring of piratical smugglers, to recovering a stolen surfboard, to tracking down a fifth-grader's missing gym shorts.
ISBN 978-1-4424-3977-1
[1. Mystery and detective stories. 2. Smuggling—Fiction. 3. Stealing—Fiction. 4. Lost and found possessions—Fiction. 5. Books and reading—Fiction. 6. Humorous stories.] I. Myers, Matthew, ill. II. Title.
PZ7.B26615Dan 2012
[Fic]—dc23
2011048401
ISBN 978-1-4424-3979-5 (eBook)

For Taylor—M. B.

CONTENTS

Contents

Steve Brixton was running out of air!

DANGER GOES BERSERK

CHAPTER I

BEGINNING AGAIN

STEVE BRIXTON, private detective, age twelve and freshly back from retirement, was reading in his office. Until last week, what was now Steve's office had been just a large doghouse in Steve Brixton's backyard, but the Brixtons did not own a dog and never had. The previous tenants had a Saint Bernard named Bandy, and when they'd moved away, they'd taken the dog but left the doghouse. Steve's mom had been using it for storage until Steve had convinced her that it was pretty much begging to be converted into the headquarters of a world-famous detective agency.

Steve had swept the place out and painted the

walls white. He'd hung up a map of Ocean Park and the surrounding coast, and he'd bought a small box of map tacks to help him keep track of crime waves. (Right now the map featured a single red pin, marking the location of the office in which the map now hung, but Steve was ready with more pins of many colors, just in case.) A small card table was Steve's desk. There were two tiny wooden chairs. In the evenings, light came from a lamp powered by a bright orange extension cord that ran across the backyard and up through Steve's bedroom window.

The space was a bit cramped, but it was clean and bright, and as long as you crouched, it could fit one comfortably—and up to two uncomfortably.

The best part: Steve had hired a professional sign painter to letter his name where the dog's name used to be—right above the door, or doorway, since there really wasn't a door, just a rectangular hole in the wall for a dog to enter and exit—and it looked like this:

And so, on a Thursday evening, Steve put his feet on his desk and read. Outside, the dark sky was shot through with peaches and pinks, and the office glowed in the dusk light. Steve's desk lamp was still unlit. He tilted back in his chair.

Behind Steve's head, on shelves he'd installed himself, were the shiny red spines of the books collectively known as the Bailey Brothers Mysteries. The Bailey Brothers Mysteries related the heart-pounding, rip-roaring adventures of Shawn and Kevin Bailey, teenage brothers, straight-A students, and red-blooded, corn-fed supersleuths. The books were by Steve's favorite author and mortal enemy, MacArthur Bart, a man who had turned to a life of crime after a long bout of writer's block. Steve had uncovered his hero's villainy when he'd discovered *The Ghostwriter Secret*—and although Steve had foiled one of Bart's schemes, the man had gotten away. It still bugged Steve that Bart was a free man. Even now Bart was no doubt incubating his sinister schemes in some dark and teeming fold of America's criminal underbelly.

Still, his books were pretty ace.

And the fact was this: Bart and the Bailey Brothers had taught Steve everything he knew about the art of detection. Steve had read and reread the fifty-eight

Bailey Brothers mysteries, plus he was deeply familiar with *The Bailey Brothers' Detective Handbook.* The handbook, which compiled the accumulated professional wisdom of Shawn and Kevin Bailey, was pretty much full-to-bursting with tricks and tips for gumshoes of all stripes. There were chapters like "Useful Morse Code" (... --- ... and -.-. .- -. -. .. -... .- .-.. ...) and "How to Outwit Hypnotists" (sing "The Star-Spangled Banner" backward).

Right now, the handbook was lying open on Steve's desk while he read Bailey Brothers #25: *The Clue of the Caves in the Cove.* The story was at a good part:

Fair-haired Kevin Bailey opened up the throttle and expertly piloted the *Deducer VII* across the rough seas. "Keep an eye out for the *Dark and Stormy!* Her black hull will be hard to spot in this pea soup!" he shouted above the roar of the speedboat's motor.

"Aye, aye!" cried dark-haired Shawn, who was manning the *Deducer VII*'s powerful search lamp. "Joseph Tanaka and his smugglers will never get away."

Their stout chum, Ernest Plumly, was

looking green. "I shouldn't have eaten such a big lunch," he groaned. "I don't know if I can ever look at a roast beef sandwich again."

"Somebody write that down!" chuckled Shawn.

"If he keeps that pledge, Albert's Delicatessen will soon be out of business!" grinned Kevin.

"Don't bet on it, fellows," Ernest rejoined with a rueful smile. "I didn't say anything about ham sandwiches."

The boys all laughed.

"Scampering squirrels!" exclaimed eagle-eyed Shawn, pointing straight ahead. "There she is! The *Dark and Stormy!*"

The smugglers' ship emerged from the fog.

Kevin got on the *Deducer VII*'s bullhorn as he slowed the boat. "Give it up, Tanaka!" he warned. "Three Coast Guard cutters are right behind us."

The hatch of the criminals' craft opened up. Joseph Tanaka popped up and shrieked, "You don't have any evidence, Baileys!" Laughing, the swarthy ringleader dumped a wooden crate into the ocean!

Quick as a flash, Shawn Bailey, who was an excellent skin diver and proficient in aquatic lifesaving techniques, dove into the choppy waters. With a few powerful strokes, he made his way toward the *Dark and Stormy*, then disappeared beneath the swells.

Many tense seconds passed as Kevin and Ernest waited for the brave sleuth to resurface.

"Sure seems like he's been down there awhile," Ernest worried.

"These are rougher seas than he's used to swimming," Kevin fretted.

Then, all of a sudden, Shawn Bailey's head broke the surface of the water. He was grinning and holding a clear bag. "Here's your evidence, Tanaka!" he exulted. He peered at the contents of the bag and read the label. "I happen to know that these are controlled pharmaceuticals! I overheard my doctor mention this particular type of medicine to a nurse last week, when I went in for my annual physical!"

"Blast you, Baileys!" Tanaka raged. The

smuggler's long black braid flapped behind him in the wind, and his gold earrings shone in the light of the *Deducer's* lamp. "Too bad you'll never make it back to shore."

"What do you mean?" Kevin queried on the bullhorn. "The *Deducer VII's* shipshape!"

"That may be so," snarled Tanaka, "but she's carrying a time bomb!"

Kevin and Ernest looked at each other in terror. *Suddenly the ticking noise they'd heard in the boathouse made sense!*

Steve turned the page just as a large figure blocked the doorway of the Brixton Brothers Detective Agency, plunging the office into darkness.

It was Danimal!

CHAPTER II

BOARD TROUBLE

"HEY, LITTLE MAN," said the big man in the doorway. Steve recognized him.

"Hi, Danimal," said Steve. "Come on in."

"New office, huh?" said Danimal, ducking through the entry. He was wearing shorts and a baggy tank top with a duck on it. His long hair was held back by sunglasses. Danimal looked around. "Place is pretty sick. Cramped, but sick. It could use a window, though."

"Well, the door's sort of the window," Steve said.

"Yeah, I guess. A real window would really open the place up, though."

"Yeah, well it used to be a doghouse."

"Right, right." Danimal looked uncomfortable, bent over at the waist and still pressed up against the ceiling.

Steve motioned for Danimal to sit. Danimal was too big for the chair. He folded his legs underneath him and sat on the floor.

"You can just put the chair outside," Steve said. It was taking up a lot of room.

"Good idea." Danimal pushed the chair through the doorway. It tipped over and fell on the lawn.

"So what's up?" Steve asked.

"I want to hire you, little man."

There wasn't room for Steve to put his feet up on the desk anymore. There was barely room for the desk. He opened up his black notebook and grabbed a pen. "What's the case?" he asked.

"Point Panic again." Point Panic was what everybody had been calling Mímulo Point, a nearby surf spot, ever since fins had been spotted offshore. Steve had first met Danimal in his last adventure, *It Happened on a Train*—the surfer had been attacked at Point Panic and his board chewed up. Steve had determined that the shark attack had been faked— although why someone would stage a bogus shark attack remained a mystery. Steve's fake-shark theory had been published in the local newspaper, and the point had recently been reopened, but lingering fear had kept the lineup sparse.

Danimal leaned forward. "So I check the surf report yesterday and I just know the point'll be going off. I strap a couple boards to the car and peel out. And as I turn the bend before Mímulo, the sun is coming up, and sure enough—corduroy out to the horizon."

Steve stopped taking notes and looked up.

"The swell," Danimal said. "Waves. Lots of them."

"Okay," said Steve.

"So I park out on the point, right behind this old ice cream truck painted like a leopard—which I already know is bad news."

"Why?"

"Truck belongs to the Berserkers. You know the Berserkers?"

Steve shook his head.

"A local surf gang. Bunch of punks. Show-offs. The leader's this guy Tremor Temchin—you ever hear of him? The story on this dude is that he's got sharks' teeth mounted on the nose of his board so that nobody drops in on him."

"Drops in?"

"Yeah," said Danimal. "Tries to surf a wave

that's his. You do that, and he'll come charging up behind you riding something sharp. The Berserkers are a pretty heavy crew. They used to hang out at Hammerhead—that's a nice break, but nobody else has surfed it for years. Everybody's afraid to. These guys are really territorial."

"Okay," Steve said.

"So I make my way down the cliffs, and when I get down to the beach, somebody's spray-painted a Viking helmet on a boulder."

"That somebody being one of the Berserkers," Steve said.

"No doubt," Danimal said. "The helmet's their logo."

Steve noted that in his book.

"So I paddle out," Danimal says. "There's already about six or seven of these Berserkers in the lineup, and when they see me coming, they start hooting at me, telling me to go home and calling me the Malman."

"The Malman?"

"A Mal's a longboard—it's an old-school board, the kind of board the guys rode in the sixties. The Berserkers are a bunch of hotdoggers—they all ride shortboards. Shortboarders are always trash-talking longboarders."

"Right," said Steve.

"So these guys start snaking my waves, dropping in on me, and edging me out of the lineup. I can't catch a ride. They're acting like Mímulo's their spot, which is nuts. I've been surfing there since I was a kid. The whole thing was bumming me out, so I paddled in after less than an hour. And when I get back up to the car, these punks have waxed my windows and stolen my other board off the roof rack."

"Waxed your windows?"

"Yeah, you rub surf wax all over the glass. Classic trick. It's a total pain to get the stuff off. But the *board*, little man. You don't steal a guy's board."

Steve took his feet off the table. He bit his thumbnail. "Why not go to the cops?" Steve asked.

"I did. They don't care. I can't prove these guys took the board," Danimal said. "But I know they did. About fifteen minutes into my session, one of the younger guys paddled in. He must have been the one who stole it. But the cops just took a crime report and said they didn't have much hope. The police here don't care what happens on the water, man."

"So you want me to be a go-between?" Steve asked. "Bargain for your board back? These guys don't sound like they're real negotiators."

"I don't care how you do it," Danimal said. "Steal

the board back, or just prove that they took it and we can take the evidence to the cops."

"Hmm," said Steve. "What does the board look like?"

"She was beautiful," Danimal said. "About ten feet long, with rounded edges. Single fin. Redwood stringer—a half-inch wood plank running down the whole length of the board. Bright red."

Steve wrote down everything Danimal said although he didn't understand most of it. When he finished, he rocked back and forth in his chair. These Berserkers were bullies, and bullies were high on the list of the Bailey Brothers' most-hated finks. (They were somewhere below cat burglars, but above safecrackers.) In fact, Shawn and Kevin mentioned how much they hated bullies in practically every Bailey Brothers book—they denounced bullies almost as often as they made jokes about Ernest eating too many sandwiches.

"Steve," Danimal said. "You have to get the board back. My grandpa shaped it himself. I love that thing." He looked near tears.

Steve stopped rocking. "I'll take your case."

CHAPTER III

HIGHWAY TO PERIL

IT WAS A SIMPLE assignment: go undercover as a surfer and prove the Berserkers had Danimal's board. If Steve gained this crew's trust, they'd probably incriminate themselves.

The Bailey Brothers' Detective Handbook has plenty of useful information about going undercover:

Shawn Bailey is a master of disguise! He's always going undercover to pump lowlifes for valuable information. We bet you won't even recognize him in these classic getups:

THE SHAGGY POET

Associates with: smugglers, political radicals, saboteurs
Lady wig
Fake beard
Turtleneck sweater
Tight slacks
Paperback novel
Favorite phrases: "hep daddy-o's," "cool cats," "the Repulsion and Attraction of Workpeople by the Factory System"

HOBO JIMMY

Associates with: smugglers, flimflam artists, other hobos
Busted hat
Dirty face
Blacked-out tooth
Bindle
Giant pants
Can of beans
Favorite phrases: "Skunk's good eatin'!," "Whatta pain in the caboose!," "I'm Hobo Jimmy!"

NUCLEAR SCIENTIST

Associates with: smugglers, Soviets, Soviet smugglers
Neat hairdo
Glasses
Lab coat
Pen
Favorite phrases: "My Atomotrons run on pure Cosmonium," "My Cosmotrons run on pure Atomium."

Unfortunately, *The Bailey Brothers' Detective Handbook* has no information on the habits and appearance of surfers. Luckily, there is plenty of insider knowledge and hip surf lingo in Bailey Brothers #54: *Death Rode the Nose*, in which the Baileys travel to Oahu, tie for first place in the Waikiki Masters Surf Tournament, and ultimately uncover a gang of kidnappers operating from beneath a volcano. After skimming the book a couple times on Thursday, Steve felt ready to hit the water.

Less ready was Dana, Steve's best chum.

"Don't call me chum," Dana said when they met up after school and got on their bikes. "Are you sure this is a good idea?"

"I'm sure it's a great idea," said Steve. "If these Berserkers respect us as surfers, they'll want to impress us by telling us about stealing Danimal's surfboard. The case will practically solve itself."

"Yeah, but we don't surf."

The boys pedaled down the road that led along the coast. Steve looked out at the ocean, windswept and white-capped, and he twinged a bit at the thought of paddling out into those gray waters. He gripped his handlebars a little tighter. *The Bailey Brothers' Detective Handbook* says, "Good gumshoes swallow their fear, then wash it down with a glass of homemade lemonade." Steve felt thirsty.

Dana had a point: They'd never been surfing. The good breaks were a decent bike ride from Ocean Park, and so neither Steve nor Dana had ever learned. Dana owned a skateboard, but Steve didn't, so Dana hardly rode it, at least not when Steve was around. And skating was different, anyway: You weren't in the ocean. Sometimes Steve would see packs of surfers huddled in the Sideways Cafe, stopping over on their way from one wave to another, or waiting out some sudden storm. There was something about the way they talked, and dressed, and moved, the way their faces were tanned even in the middle of winter, that made them seem unapproachable. The surfers Steve had seen in town never looked like they fully belonged on land.

The bike lane narrowed as they left Ocean Park, and the cars drove faster now. The boys wound around curves, past cliff sides and boulders, the ocean always sprawling on their right. Soon they were heading down a long and gentle grade, going so fast that they didn't have to pedal. Up ahead, a stone bridge crossed a stream that trickled onto the beach. Without either of them saying anything, Steve and Dana agreed to race to the other side.

The chain on Steve's bike clicked as he shifted up several gears. He pedaled hard. Dana was already ahead, but Steve was gaining ground. Dana looked back to size up his lead, and Steve saw a big grin on his best chum's face. They were really going now: Steve could feel the hairs on his forearms blowing in the wind. Dana made it onto the bridge, and then Steve, the gap between the boys really shrinking now. Riding on stone was rougher than pavement. Steve got up to within a foot of Dana's back tire.

Before the boys were halfway across the bridge, a black convertible came racing up behind them, careening into the bike lane!

CHAPTER IV

SURF SCENE

Tires squealed. Metal screamed. Steve, then Dana, fell off his bike. The car swerved back into its lane, tapped on the brakes long enough for its driver to verify that the boys were unhit and alive, then sped wildly down the road. Steve pushed himself up on one knee, shielded his eyes, and squinted. The car was a black Lamborghini. Its driver was bald, and there was another man in the passenger seat. Steve could just make out the car's rear license plate:

DROMOND

Another brush with death!

Steve whipped out his notebook and wrote the license down, even though he doubted he'd forget it. This guy was going to pay. He snapped the notebook shut and returned it to his shorts. Dana was standing up, examining a skinned knee. Steve brushed some pebbles from a scrape on his left palm.

"You all right?" Dana asked.

"Yeah. You?"

"Yeah. Who was that guy?"

Steve patted his back pocket. "We'll find out."

They picked up their bikes and walked them across the bridge in silence. Steve's heart was still pounding away, and his mind was busy replaying the near accident.

After they'd walked for about a quarter mile, the boys' nerves settled, and they got on their bikes. Steve and Dana rode south. Ten minutes later they pulled up in front of a surf shop. The building stood alone on the road, across the street from the ocean. It was painted lime green, and one wall bore the name of the store—Swells—next to the image of a cresting wave. Steve and Dana went inside.

The shop smelled like neoprene and grape surf wax. A punk song pumped through speakers in the ceiling competed with a punk song blaring from the TV—the store was full of frantic drumming and guitars. The floor held mostly clothing racks stocked with shirts and shorts. There were shoes on one wall, including a pair of sandals that looked like they were made of Astroturf. Surfboards stood in a rack at the back of the shop.

The only other person in the store was the guy behind the counter. He was about seventeen, with bleached white hair that got dark at the roots. One long sleeve of his T-shirt was rolled up, and his chin rested on his folded forearms. He was watching a video of people riding huge waves.

"Aloha, dude," said Steve.

The clerk swung his head around and took in Steve and Dana.

"Hey. Can I help you guys?"

"Totally. We'd like to be outfitted like a couple of professional surfers from the Hawaiian Islands."

The clerk looked at Steve. "Okay."

Steve looked at the clerk.

"Um," said the clerk, "what do you need?"

"Like I said, we're going out surfing today, and we want to rent the best pro gear."

"So a couple boards and a couple steamers?"

"Uh-huh," Steve said.

"You wear a four-three or a three-two?"

"Depends," said Steve.

The clerk looked confused. "Well, which do you want?"

"Well," said Steve, thinking. "That's a very good question." He thought some more. "I'm sorry. What are we talking about?"

"Wetsuits."

"Right." Steve mulled that over. "Are those also called steamers?"

"Have you guys ever been surfing before?"

"No."

The guy got up and walked around the counter. He pulled two black wetsuits from a plastic container. They were inside out—the clerk reached into their neck holes, one at a time, and reversed them, then held them with outstretched arms. "First, you guys are gonna need some suits."

"Okay," said Dana.

Steve scrunched his mouth. "Hmmm," he said. "I think we need something flashier."

"Flashier?" said the clerk.

"Yeah," said Steve. He pointed to a poster on the wall that showed a surfer flying off the lip of a foaming wave. Spray fanned off the back of his board like a rooster tail, perfectly framing the surfer's wild hair and electric-yellow wetsuit.

The clerk laughed. "All right. Let me see what I can find, bro."

He disappeared through a door marked EMPLOYEES ONLY and returned with a hot-pink wetsuit. The logo was wearing off, and the color was faded in parts, but it was much better than the drab thing this guy had just tried to pass off on Steve.

"So there's this . . . ," said the clerk.

"Looks good," said Steve. "Do you have another one for my chum?"

"Uh, this one is pretty much one-of-a-kind."

Probably because all the other flashy suits were already rented out by surfers who had gotten there first thing in the morning. Steve looked at Dana. "I should probably wear that one, since I'll be taking the lead out there."

"That's fine," Dana said.

"It might be a little small," said the clerk.

"I'll try it on," said Steve, heading to a dressing room. "But I bet it'll work."

It was a little small. Steve had to pull the suit mightily to get it over his legs. He contorted to get his arms into the sleeves. It was like wearing a rubber band. But after jumping up and down a few times to get his body situated in the thing, he was able to zip it up. A little small, but small was good. Steve was pretty sure pro surfers preferred small wetsuits—the better to show off their muscles. He looked in a full-length mirror and flexed. Ace.

Steve stepped out of the dressing room.

Ace!

Dana looked concerned. "I'm not sure that suit is the best for undercover work."

"What are you talking about?" said Steve.

"Well, that suit is kind of . . . bright. Isn't the point of undercover work to be low-key and not obvious?" Dana asked.

"No. That's *surveillance* work. The point of undercover work is to blend in."

"That's what I just said," Dana said.

"No, because today we want to blend in with a crowd that is definitely not low-key. Dana, we are going undercover as the most radical surfers. Get it? That's why this wetsuit is so good. The most radical surfers wear wetsuits like this. Look around at the photos in this place."

"I guess," Dana said.

"You guess?" Steve turned to the guy behind the counter. "Hey, don't the most radical surfers wear wetsuits like this?"

The guy looked up from a magazine and gave Steve a once-over and grinned. "Sure, dude," he said. "Definitely." He went back to reading.

"It's just too bad they don't have another one for you," Steve told Dana.

"Yeah . . ."

"Hey, dude," said Steve to the clerk. "We're ready for some boards."

The clerk put down his magazine and showed them to the rental boards. "Since it's your first time out, I'll set you guys up on a couple longboards."

"No way," Steve said. "The guys we're trying to blend in with are shortboarders," he explained to Dana. "Danimal said shortboarders are always talking trash about longboarders."

"Look," said the clerk. "If you want to stand up today, you're going to want a longboard."

"I want that one," Steve said, pointing to a bright white board with a red bull's-eye inside a blue ring.

The clerk shrugged. "Suit yourself."

"I think I'll take a longboard," Dana said.

Steve turned to his chum. "Dana! We've got to look like pros out there!"

"Then we should at least have a chance of standing up."

"We can stand up," Steve said. "How hard can this be? Kevin Bailey did a headstand on his first day out in the water."

"Look, bro," said the clerk, "I don't know who Kevin Bailey is, but if he was doing headstands, he must have been riding a longboard. No way you can do that on a shortboard. Noseriding, boardwalking, you want a longboard for all that stuff."

"Well, I already have a boring wetsuit," Dana said. "So maybe I should just ride a boring board, too."

"All right," said Steve. "Fine. I'll just say you're an old-school Hawaiian-style surfer."

"So you guys ready to check out?" the clerk said.

Steve paid for the suits and boards, and left a deposit in case the gear was lost or damaged.

"So you guys have never been out before?" the clerk asked after he filled out a receipt.

Dana shook his head.

"All right, look, I'll give you a little lesson."

The three went to a clear area of floor in the front of the store. The clerk stood behind the two boys. "First you need to figure out whether you ride regular foot or goofy-foot."

"What's that?" Dana asked.

"It's what foot you put forward when you stand up. If you put your left foot forward, you're regular foot."

"How do we figure that out?"

The clerk shoved Steve in the back.

Steve caught himself with his right foot.

"You're goofy," said the clerk.

Steve felt miffed.

"How about me?" Dana asked.

"Get down on your belly and push yourself up like you're standing up on a wave."

When Dana raised up into a crouch, his left foot was in front.

"You're regular foot," said the clerk.

"Why didn't you push him?" Steve asked.

"If you surf regular foot, you'll probably like waves that break to the right, because that way you can face the wave. Goofy-footers like to go left."

"Okay, but why didn't you push Dana?"

"All right, next up." The clerk grabbed the long rubber leash coming off the back of Dana's board. "Attach this leash to your back leg. That way your board won't get lost in the water."

The boys nodded.

"Now, when you paddle out there, get past where the waves are breaking and face away from the shore. When you see a swell coming—there'll be the bumps in the ocean coming at you—turn your board around by kicking your legs like eggbeaters. Get down on your belly and start paddling hard. If you feel the wave take you, push yourself up and go."

That sounded simple enough.

"Try it," said the clerk. He pointed to the floor. "Get down there and pretend that a wave is coming."

Steve and Dana lay on the floor.

"Paddle, paddle, paddle!" the clerk shouted. Steve paddled on the carpet. He felt dumb.

"Now stand."

He pushed himself up and struck a pose like Kevin

Bailey's on the cover of *Death Rode the Nose*. It still felt dumb.

"You should probably watch the other surfers out there for a while to see how they do it. Where are you thinking of going out? Cowry Cove is a nice little beginner's break."

Steve shook his head. "We're surfing Mímulo Point," he said.

The clerk's eyes grew wide. His mouth dropped open.

"You know, Point Panic," said Steve.

"You must be joking," said the clerk. "You're going to get yourselves killed."

CHAPTER V

POINT PANIC

IT WAS HARD BALANCING on a bike with a surfboard under your arm, but Steve felt cool doing it, even when he wobbled. The sun was low in the west, and a hazy layer of fog was beginning to settle over the coast, but Steve was already sweating in his wetsuit. The boys rode to the base of Mímulo Point, a long peninsula about two miles south of Swells Surf Shop. They chained their bikes to a wooden sign detailing the habits and characteristics of the long-billed curlew, and stashed their shoes and backpacks behind some rocks.

There was only one car parked on the shoulder

of the highway: a dented ice cream truck painted orange with black spots. Spray-painted on the back, in unruly green letters, were the words "SURF BERSERK."

Steve went over to the truck and peeked through a grimy window. The back held a mattress, some clothes, a couple dirty plates, and many surfboards. The boards were all zipped up in silver board bags— they looked like giant hot dogs wrapped in tinfoil. The longest of them was big enough to be Danimal's longboard, but there was no way of telling without getting in the van and opening up that bag. Too bad—that would have been easy.

Steve joined Dana at the edge of the point. Shoulder to shoulder, the boys looked down at the water. Waves were breaking off the point, peeling gently to the right. There were eight guys on boards out in the water. Steve watched their technique. It was just like the guy in the surf shop had said: They paddled down the face of the wave, stood, and turned. The waves, thankfully, did not look too big— most were about as high as the waists of the riders. Some of the surfers zagged up and down the face of the wave, snapping the board around at the lip. One guy used the wave like a ramp, launching himself into the air and grabbing his board. Sometimes the cheers of the surfers were audible even from atop the palisade.

"That doesn't look too hard," Steve said.

"The guy in the shop said we were going to die," said Dana.

"Yeah, that guy didn't know what he was talking about."

"I think he did know what he was talking about. He works in a surf shop. The whole point is that he know what he's talking about."

"He was probably just trying to sell us surf lessons or something."

"He said if the rocks didn't get us, the Berserkers would."

Steve pointed to a group of black rocks that jutted up where the wave ended. "Well, there are the rocks. As long as we stay away from those, we only have the Berserkers to worry about."

The surfers hooted for a rider who spun around like a propeller as he crashed down a wave into the whitewater.

"Let's do this," Steve said.

They picked their way down the path on the cliff, avoiding sharp stones and broken bottles. Occasionally Steve's board would whack Dana's board, and there would be a thud that did not sound at all good.

The dirt path ended in a field of black rocks—past those, the beach.

Steve followed Dana's path across the rocks, wincing every time he put his foot in the wrong place. He was relieved to reach the sand.

"There it is," Steve said, pointing to a boulder that bore the stenciled image of a horned helmet. "The Berserkers."

They walked on to the water's edge. The waves looked farther away from down here—they'd have to paddle a while to get over to the pack of surfers. None of the Berserkers seemed to have noticed them yet.

Steve stared at the water. It was gray. The water was gray and the sand was gray, and the rocks were black. Steve was already cold—the breeze chilled the sweat on his neck above the wetsuit—and the water looked freezing. Freezing and wet and somehow unfriendly. And gray.

This was maybe a bad idea.

Steve let an incoming wave envelop his legs up to the calf. An icy shock hit the bones in his toes as his feet sank into the sand. The wave pulled back, and grains of sand tickled his soles. Steve was acutely aware of the air around his ankles. The cold was painful.

Dana was hopping up and down on the beach, his huge board diagonal under one arm. "Okay, okay, okay," he was saying over and over to himself. Then he let out a small scream and ran for the water. Steve screamed too, and followed his chum into the ocean.

CHAPTER VI

PADDLE OUT

BELLY DOWN ON HIS BOARD, Steve felt dwarfed by the waves. What had looked like mounds from the beach were mountains in the sea. A wall of whitewater came crashing toward Steve's face. It was like being slapped by a frozen fish. He tasted salt in his mouth. Frigid seawater had made its way inside his suit, and the wind whipped his hair. Dana was already ten yards ahead, paddling through the soupy beach break. Steve stood (the water was knee-deep here), picked up his board, and ran straight for the rushing white-water. He slapped his board onto the sea and began paddling furiously. Each oncoming wave seemed to bring him back to where he started, but when Steve looked back over his shoulder, he saw that he'd made some progress: The beach was far behind him.

Eventually Steve made it out past the whitewater to where the waves peaked and broke. Sometimes he'd paddle over the lip and come shooting down the trough on the other side. Other times a breaker would fling Steve backward and crash on top of him. Steve would then abandon his board and dive underwater, taking refuge in the freezing depths, listening to the thundering wave overhead. His leash would tug at his ankle as the wave dragged his board shoreward, and Steve had to struggle to swim against the force. When he could hold his breath no longer, Steve would try to resurface, disoriented and blinded by the daylight. And always, always, there were more waves. Steve would pull his board toward him, get on, and paddle once again.

Finally Steve joined Dana out past the breaking waves. Something had gone wrong. The boys had paddled out with their boards pointed right at the Berserkers. But the current had pulled them far to the south, and now the surfers looked tiny in the distance. Steve couldn't imagine having the strength to paddle his way all the way over to them.

He and Dana caught their breath as they sat on

their boards, bobbing up and down on the rolling swells. The sun was now below the clouds, low and red in the west.

"That was awful," Steve said. He could feel his nose running but didn't know whether it was snot or seawater.

"Yeah," said Dana.

"My arms are burning," said Steve.

Dana shrugged. "We've already made it this far."

"Yeah," said Steve. They paddled toward the Berserkers.

CHAPTER VII

OUT OF LIMITS

THE SURFERS WATCHED the boys approach. Waves passed
unridden. Nobody said anything.

As Steve got closer to the pack, he noticed that the
biggest of the eight Berserkers wore a metal Viking
helmet on his head. Two great horns protruded from
the sides, and in the afternoon light the helmet glowed
like it was on fire. The effect was unsettling.

Another Berserker was wearing a chimp mask.
That was maybe even more unsettling than the Viking
helmet.

Actually, the chimp mask was definitely more
unsettling than the Viking helmet.

None of the crew seemed happy to see the boys. Every face was frowning, except for the chimp face, which was smiling, but that was just the mask. It was impossible to know what the face beneath the mask was doing. But probably frowning.

While they were still out of the Berserkers' earshot, Steve stopped paddling and whispered to Dana. "I almost forgot. We need surf names."

"What?"

"Did you not hear my whisper or did you not understand?"

"I didn't understand."

"Surf names."

"I know. I said I heard you."

"Well I don't understand how you don't understand."

"What's a surf name?"

"You know, nicknames that we use after we leave our land names behind and follow the sun and waves forever. Every great surfer has a surf name. When Shawn and Kevin go to Hawaii, they befriend a surf bum named Bonzo Dog who shows them around the islands. Bonzo Dog is pretty much the greatest surfer on Oahu."

"So what's your surf name?" Dana asked.

"I'm Bull's-eye."

"Who are you?"

"Bull's-eye?"

Steve gestured to the logo on his board. "Yeah, it'll make it look like this was designed specifically for me."

"Oh, because of that target?"

"Yeah, but it's a bull's-eye, not a target."

"It's the same thing."

"Look. I'm not going to call myself Target."

"Okay," said Dana. "Then what's my surf name?"

"You're Tubesnake."

"What?"

"Yeah!"

"Tubesnake?"

"Tubesnake!"

"I don't know . . ."

"What are you talking about? That's a great surf name! Actually, maybe I should be Tubesnake." Steve thought it over. "Oh, right, I can't. Because of my board."

"Why can't I just be Dana? You know, to go with the wetsuit, and the longboard."

Steve shook his head. "Fine, but these guys aren't going to respect you at all." He started paddling again. "Follow my lead out there."

Steve and Dana made their way into the lineup. Steve sat up on his board and made a hang-loose sign with the thumb and pinkie of his right hand.

"Aloha, dudes! My chum and I would like to join your surf gang. Can I talk to the big kahuna?"

The chimp spoke. "Who are you?"

"Oh, we're just a couple of pro surfers from the Hawaiian Islands. The guy here on the dumb longboard is Dana, and my name is Bull's-eye Tubesnake."

The chimp looked at the man in the helmet. "Are these guys for real, Trem?"

Trem! Short for Tremor, no doubt. The big guy was the head Berserker. Steve gave him a closer look. He looked tall, although it was hard to say while he was on his board. Broad-shouldered. Barrel-chested. His hair was blond and his wetsuit black. His eyes were cool blue and trained on Steve. Tremor rode a green board, but it was unlike any Steve had ever seen. Jagged white teeth were mounted on the board's blunt nose, and it seemed that Tremor was astride some kind of cruelly grimacing beast.

Steve had to play it low-key. Let Tremor come to him.

Tremor didn't say anything.

They bobbed up and down on their boards in silence. There was the sound of gulls and the sound of the waves. Steve examined the faces of the surfers around him—they were in their late teens and early twenties, some with long hair, some with buzz cuts. The meanest of the bunch had bright green hair and seemed both angry and shocked that Steve was in the water—his mouth was open so wide that Steve could see a nasty-looking piercing through his tongue. Steve didn't like the way this guy was staring at him, but then again, all the surfers were staring at him. Steve gave a friendly nod in the Berserkers' general direction and looked down.

The sea was a blue so dark it was almost black, and Steve couldn't see his legs underwater. He pictured his toes, pink and wriggling a couple feet below his board. What else was going on down there? He pictured stingrays gliding by, trailing barbed and poisonous tails. Black urchins shooting spines out in all directions. Maybe a moray eel was even now eyeing Steve's calf. Its mouth gaped, its teeth eager to tear through flesh. An armored lobster was swimming up to snip off Steve's big toe. Could lobsters swim? Octopuses. Jellyfish. Great white sharks. Waters this black could hide a great white shark—could hide a hundred great white sharks—unblinking, hungry, circling closer and closer. The brutes would strike at any second.

Steve took his legs out of the water and put them up on his board. He almost tipped over. It was time to move this along.

"So," Steve said. "Any of you guys hang ten today? Me, personally, I just like hanging five. I mean, I'm great at hanging ten and everything, but it just seems so showy. You dudes know what I mean, bros?"

Nothing.

"Of course," continued Steve, "my favorite thing to do when I'm out here surfing is shooting the curl. Oh man. I really love shooting the curl."

"That's enough," Tremor said.

Steve went quiet.

Tremor smiled. He had a nice smile. "You guys are from Hawaii, huh?"

"Yep," Steve said.

"Which island?"

"Oh." Steve tried to think of the best answer. "I'm from Oahu. Dana is from Maui. But now he lives on Oahu. He moved to Oahu, what was it, five years ago?"

"Six," Dana said.

Nice one, Dana.

"I head out to the islands every year," said Tremor. "What's your favorite restaurant on the North Shore?"

Steve panicked. He didn't know any restaurants on the North Shore. He wasn't entirely sure what the North Shore was. "I like them all," he said. "Hey, did you know that *aloha* means both 'hello' and 'good-bye'?"

"Yeah, I'd heard that," Tremor said. "So. Why should I let you guys become Berserkers?"

"Because we're really ace surfers. Last year Dana and I tied for first in the Waikiki Masters."

Tremor scratched his head up near where his hair met the helmet. "That's funny. There's no such thing as the Waikiki Masters."

The Berserkers all laughed.

"That's it, I'm outta here," said the green-haired surfer. He turned his board toward the beach and started paddling. He spat in Steve's direction, and Steve could hear the piercing hit his two front teeth. "Kook patrol."

"Wait," Steve said. "We're really good. We always—"

"Listen," Tremor said. No warmth remained in his face. "Maybe you haven't heard of us. But this is our break. The Berserkers surf Point Panic, and nobody else. Definitely not kooks like you. You shouldn't be here now, and you should never come back again."

"Thanks for the warning," Steve said, "but—"

"No." Tremor was very still. Steve hadn't noticed till now, but the rest of the Berserkers had drifted into a half circle behind him. "You're wrong. This isn't a warning."

"Aloha, dudes," said Steve. "We'd like to become Berserkers."

Tremor turned and nodded.

Steve's eye was drawn to a flash of light.

The chimp had a diver's knife in his right hand and was paddling, quickly but quietly, toward Dana.

Dana didn't see the chimp coming up behind him—he was still watching Tremor.

Steve screamed his chum's name and leapt into the water. But the chimp had already lunged.

CHAPTER VIII

BANZAI WASHOUT

THE BAILEY BROTHERS' DETECTIVE HANDBOOK has some nifty advice about aquatic combat:

Shawn and Kevin Bailey fight crime on land, at sea, and in the air! (And also under the ground, in venues such as abandoned silver mines, makeshift smuggling tunnels, and, of course, sea caves, *which are both underwater and underground!*) But the brothers' favorite place to battle baddies is probably in the water. The Baileys are excellent skin divers as well as co-captains of the varsity swim team. And a good thing too! Whether their seaplane crashes or their speedboat explodes, it seems these sleuths are always ending up in the drink! One of Kevin's favorite moves is to dive deep and swim over to a foe. The key is holding his breath so the baddie can't see the bubbles coming toward him.

When Kevin surfaces, he surprises the goon with a knuckle sandwich! He's like a human dolphin!

Underwater, Steve couldn't hear what was happening above. He swam through the blackness toward Dana, holding his breath and kicking. The water was cold, and Steve felt the cold all around and all through him. The space above his nose ached—it was like someone had driven an icicle between his eyes. He swam on.

His strokes were getting sloppy, his kicking froglike. Steve was running out of breath. He'd lost track of where he was going. His lungs twisted in his rib cage. He'd need to surface. Hopefully he was within punching distance of the chimp.

Steve resurfaced in the midst of the Berserkers. Everybody was moving, shouting. Where was Dana?

Steve couldn't see his chum or the chimp.

"Outside!" a surfer shouted.

"Outside!"

It was like they'd coordinated it: All at once, the Berserkers whipped their boards around, out toward the sea. Steve was treading water, frantically trying to get his bearings.

"Outside!"

The surfers paddled west. Steve watched. Should he follow them? Was this a trap? What did "outside" mean?

And then Steve saw it: three huge bumps on the water, rolling his way. The surfers had been lined up out past the breakers, but this set was cresting early. Helplessly, Steve began to swim after the Berserkers, but he already knew it was too late. A wave, bigger than any other he'd seen today, was rising from the ocean. There was no way he'd make it up the face and over the back. Steve turned around and tried to swim back to the beach—hopefully he could out-run it just a bit, make it out of the impact zone. But before he even started swimming, Steve was sucked up the face of the wave and slammed back down to the water.

Darkness again. And cold. And panic. Steve did a backflip beneath the surface. He swallowed a mouthful of seawater. It burned his throat. He needed air. Steve kicked and flailed—the surface couldn't be far away now. His hand hit something hard. He reached out. Sand. The ocean floor. He'd been swimming in the wrong direction. He twisted around in the blackness, put both feet on the bottom, and propelled himself upward.

He resurfaced. It took a second to adjust. It was bright, and things around him seemed to be moving fast. Steve gasped. He looked over his shoulder to see another wave crashing down behind him.

The last thing Steve saw before he ducked below the water was his board flying through the air. He knew it would hit him two seconds before it actually did. Steve felt a sharp pain above his left eye, but there was no time to worry about that now. Something was pulling on his ankle. There was tension on the leash. Steve let himself be dragged—feet, yards— behind his board.

He was surrounded by froth now, safe in the shallows. He stood and put a hand up to his forehead. It came back red with blood. Steve was dazed. There was sand in his mouth, and his teeth ground against the grit when he clenched his jaw. He had a headache.

Dana.

Steve called out Dana's name. He was out of breath and struggled to make his voice louder than the surf.

There was no answer.

He shouted Dana's name again.

CHAPTER IX

WASH UP

"Steve!"

The cry came from far away. Steve turned and saw his chum standing on the shore, halfway down the beach.

Steve picked up his board and took off down the sand. The waves erased the long line of footprints he left behind him.

Steve was exhausted by the time he reached Dana. He was glad to see his chum alive. Dana looked okay—he didn't appear to have any knife wounds, but those would probably be hard to see under the wetsuit.

"Hey," said Dana, weakly. He had sand in his black hair.

"Dana," said Steve. "Did the chimp stab you?"

"Did the what what me?"

"The chimp. Did he stab you?"

"Oh. That guy. What do you mean, stab me?"

"Dana! He had a knife!"

"He did?"

"How did you miss that?"

"Well, I can't see behind me, Steve."

"You have to see behind you, especially in times of danger. Kevin Bailey always says, 'Not only do sleuths need eyes in the back of their heads—those eyes need to have twenty-twenty vision.'"

"Well, that's dumb," Dana said.

"How is that dumb?"

"Because twenty-twenty vision means you can see at twenty feet what a normal person can see at twenty feet. And since a normal person can't see anything behind them at twenty feet, then technically I do have twenty-twenty vision from the back of my head."

"Now, *that's* dumb," Steve said.

"What happened to your head?" Dana asked. "The chimp?"

Steve wished the chimp had stabbed him. That

would have been way more ace than getting hit by a falling surfboard. "I got hurt trying to save you," Steve said. "Where'd you go?"

"I don't know. I got knocked off my board by something, I guess a wave—"

"Probably the chimp!" Steve said. "He attacked you!"

"Well, then I got caught up in that monster set. It was crazy. And then the current took me over by those rocks, and I thought I was going to get impaled, but I, like, pushed off that big rock over there, and then I swam here."

Steve checked his chum one last time for knife wounds, head to toe. Everything looked normal. Except—

"Where's your board?" Steve asked. Steve pointed to Dana's ankle. His leash wasn't attached to anything.

"I don't know," said Dana. "My leash must have snapped on the rocks. Do you see it out there?"

"Dana! Don't you see? The chimp cut your leash. The Berserkers stole another board."

"You think?" Dana said. The boys looked out to the lineup. The surfers had arranged themselves in a circle, and they were all watching the beach. Behind them, the sun dipped into the ocean. There must have been some sort of signal: At once, all the surfers put their hands up to their heads, extending their pinkies to look like the horns on a Viking helmet— all except for Tremor, who already had the headgear, and whose hands rested on his waist. The Berserkers let out tremendous bellows. The water carried their war cries to the beach.

"Your board's probably in the middle of that circle," Steve said.

Dana looked furious. "We gotta get those guys!" He was ready to charge out to sea.

Steve put a hand on his chum's shoulder. "Wait. There are too many of them now, and at least one of them's got a knife."

"But they have my board!" Dana said.

"Well, technically, I paid the deposit on it," said Steve.

"Oh. Right."

Steve grabbed a clump of wet sand. This was not how the afternoon was supposed to go. By now they should have already been invited to the Berserkers' luau. "You guys ever steal any boards from Malmen?" Steve would ask as they were paddling to shore in the sunset. "All the time," Tremor would say. "We got this nice red board from a kook just the other day. Want to see it?" They'd go up to the truck, Tremor would unzip the board bag, and boom, Steve would place him under citizen's arrest.

Instead Steve's forehead was bleeding and his stomach was full of seawater. The Berserkers were out there laughing at them. And they'd stolen one of their boards.

Wait.

That was it.

Steve had them.

The Berserkers had stolen a board! They'd pulled a knife on Dana and stolen a surfboard. That was a crime. Two crimes. Steve could paddle back out there and put them all under citizen's arrest right now.

He remembered the knife.

"Come on." Steve grimaced. "We have to go to the cops."

It was getting hard to see by the time they got back up the palisade. Steve retrieved his backpack and the boys got on their bikes. Something was wrong.

Steve's pedals spun, but his bike didn't move. Dana wasn't getting anywhere either. Steve looked down. Somebody had stolen their chains.

"You've got to be joking me," Steve said.

Dana just stood next to his bike and shook his head.

"It was that green-haired one, the guy who pad-dled in. Probably the same guy who stole Danimal's board." Steve dismounted and unzipped his back-pack. He pulled out a tin of cocoa mix and a pair of pink dishwashing gloves.

"This is good," Steve said. He applied the cocoa powder to the frame of his bike. "This is actually good. We'll see if we can get a set of fingerprints, then I'll bring those to Chief Clumber, and then we can add bicycle theft to the list of their crimes."

"Uh, Steve," said Dana, "I think you're wasting your time."

Steve now had a flashlight in his mouth. "Evidence collection is never a waste of time," he said. Or that's what he meant to say. It came out, "Emidesh com-memmton ith nemm a waamm eyem."

"What?" said Dana.

Steve removed the flashlight. "Evidence collection is never a waste of time, Dana. The handbook, page three. I might be able to link a Berserker with this theft. That goon thought he could get away with this, but we'll prove it was him."

"I don't think that's a big secret." Dana pointed to a piece of a paper speared on his handlebar.

Steve snatched the paper and shone his flashlight on it.

Kooks, go home.

Steve crumpled up the paper and threw it on the ground. Then he picked it back up, smoothed it out, and put it in a ziplock bag. He took a Sharpie from his backpack's outside pouch and labeled the bag EXHIBIT A.

"This means war," Steve said.

CHAPTER X

POLICE EMERGENCY

TWO HOURS LATER Steve and Dana walked their bikes up to the front door of the Ocean Park Police Station. (Steve had hidden his board in a ditch by the highway—it was too heavy to carry all the way back to town.)

They burst through the entrance. Officer Johnson was on duty behind the front desk, staring at a newspaper and scratching his temple with the tip of a pencil.

"Good evening, Officer Johnson," said Steve, all business.

"Hi, Steve!" Johnson seemed happy to see him.

"I need to see Chief Clumber," Steve said. "Now."

Johnson frowned. "Oh, well, this is a bad time, Steve. He's busy."

Steve shook his head. "Trust me: Clumber's gonna want to hear about this."

Johnson stood up, but Steve had already passed his desk and was walking back through the station. Dana squeezed by the desk sergeant and offered an apologetic shrug. They walked by a set of empty desks and up a flight of stairs. A narrow hallway ended in a door marked CHIEF FRANK CLUMBER.

"Let me do the talking in here," Steve said. He knocked and, without waiting, turned the knob and barged inside.

There were four men in the room. One was Chief Clumber. Two were strangers in cheap suits. The fourth was Rick.

Great.

Rick was Steve's mom's boyfriend, a sergeant with the OPPD, and the owner of a blond mustache. He was also a jerk.

"Clumber," said Steve, "we need to talk."

It was hard to say which man was most perplexed by Steve's entrance. They all looked equally confused, except for Rick, who just looked annoyed.

"Who's this?" asked one of the strangers.

"I'm Steve Brixton, and I'm a private detective. Who are you?"

"Steve," said Chief Clumber. "Now isn't the time. I'm busy."

"I can see that," Steve said, "but you'll want to hear what I have to tell you. There's an emergency."

Clumber sighed. He checked the faces of the two men in suits, who remained expressionless. "What is it?" the chief asked.

"A bunch of guys stole Dana's rental surfboard and took the chains off our bikes."

Silence followed Steve's sentence. He was pleased: Word of the crimes had the crowd speechless.

"And?" Clumber asked.

"And it's justice time," Steve said.

Clumber rested his big head in his hands. "Leave," he said. "Now."

Rick smirked.

"But, Chief," said Steve.

"Now," said Clumber.

Steve and Dana backed out of the office.

Steve shook his head. "I can't believe they're in there gabbing while the trail gets cold."

The boys waited downstairs. Officer Johnson made them hot chocolate and let them use the desk phone to call their parents. Steve told his mom where he was but omitted the details likely to upset her, which were most of them.

They waited on the first floor. Steve sat in Rick's chair, Dana on Rick's desk. Dana was saying something about their adventure in the water, but Steve wasn't paying attention. He was staring at a photograph, crooked in a silver frame, of his mom and Rick on a pier. Steve turned the frame facedown. Then he picked it back up and put it in its right place. Dana had stopped talking and was watching Steve. For a while neither boy said anything.

Steve had his head down on the desk and was close to falling asleep when the two men in suits walked through the precinct room. Neither man acknowledged Steve, which struck him as lacking in professional courtesy.

Johnson's phone rang as the men were exiting the station.

"Guys," Johnson said, returning the receiver to the cradle, "Clumber's ready for you."

"Okay," Steve said to Dana. "*Now* it's justice time."

CHAPTER XI

DEAD END

IT WAS CROWDED on the other side of Clumber's desk—
Steve, Dana, and Rick were arrayed in metal chairs
before the chief. It was crowded on Clumber's side
of the desk too, but that was just Clumber. Chief
Clumber was a large man—too big for his chair, and
also his uniform.

Steve and Dana had just finished relaying their
encounter with the Berserkers, starting with Danimal
and ending with the broken bikes.

Clumber had his eyes closed, either absorbing the
information or taking a nap. The chief's silence gave
Rick the opportunity to talk first.

"Wait, so you guys went surfing?" he said.

"Yeah," said Steve.

"Did you catch any waves?"

"That wasn't the point," Steve said. "It was an undercover assignment."

"That's a no," said Rick. "You should have told me what you were up to. I could have given you some pointers."

"You know how to surf?" Dana said.

"Oh, sure, sure. I was pretty heavily into the whole scene, back in the day," Rick said, stroking his mustache. "Lived out of my van for a few years, just looking for waves—and beach babes! Don't tell your mom."

"Sounds great," Steve said.

"Anyway, I can't believe you thought you were going to convince these guys you were pros." Rick snorted. "Surfing is a lifestyle, guys. You've got to have soul." He pointed to his sternum. "Right here," he said.

"Uh-huh," said Steve.

"Is it stuffy in here?" Clumber asked, his eyes open now.

"A little," said Dana.

"Probably because there are so many people," Steve said.

"Rick, open the window," said Clumber.

"Or Rick could just leave," said Steve. "I don't see why—"

"All right, Steve. I've had a long day. I listened to your story. Now what do you want me to do?"

"What do I want you to—come on, Chief! Arrest these guys and put them in the slammer!"

Rick snorted. "Hate to break it to you, Stevie, but people don't usually do hard time for vandalism."

Clumber nodded. "Rick's right. A couple bicycle chains, we're talking about a small fine, if that. Probably just community service."

"What about the boards?"

"What about them?"

"These guys stole two surfboards."

"Did you get the proof that they took"—he looked down at his notes—"Danimal's board?"

Steve slouched. "No."

"And Dana, you didn't see anyone take your board, right?"

"Yeah, that's true," Dana said. "I was underwater."

"Oh, come on! The chimp cut his leash."

"Did you see this happen?" Clumber asked.

"No, but—"

"Leashes snap," Rick said.

"But the chimp had a knife!"

"When I was surfing," Rick said, "I wouldn't even use a leash. A good waterman knows how to take care of his board out on the water. That's how we used to do it. If your board got away from you, you went after it. I remember this one time, it must have been double overhead and there was this monster riptide. I was the only one who'd paddled out that day—my buddy had taken one look at these waves and gone back home, no thanks, too nuts for me, see you tomorrow—and I'd just gotten—"

"Why is Rick here?" Steve asked.

"Because we were doing real police work before you came," Rick said, "and we've got real police work to do after you leave."

"Real police would be down there putting cuffs on the Berserkers right now," Steve said.

Chief Clumber interrupted. "Look, Steve. Mímulo Point isn't even in our jurisdiction. That's the county boys."

"Fine," said Steve. "Then can you call in a favor with someone in the county sheriff's office?"

"No."

"Okay. Could you give me the name and phone number of someone at the county I can trust?"

"No."

"Unbelievable."

"I know this feels important to you, Steve, but you have to understand that this is small-time stuff. And we don't have time right now to go chase down a couple surf bums."

"Danimal's right," Steve said. "You guys don't care what happens on the water."

Clumber reddened. He leaned over his desk. "Don't give me that garbage. Now, I've listened to you, Steve, and I've tried to understand your situation. But I don't need some hotshot private detective coming in here and telling me how to do my job. I don't care about what happens on the water? For your information, the Ocean Park Police Department is assisting in an investigation of the biggest piracy-slash-smuggling case this country's seen in a century."

CHAPTER XII

ANOTHER MYSTERY

SMUGGLING IS THE SUBJECT of nineteen of the fifty-eight Bailey Brothers mysteries, more than any other crime, ahead of sabotage (twelve) and kidnapping millionaires (seven). There are only two Bailey Brothers books where the baddies are pirates—less common villains than even hoboes or amnesiacs—but both those books are pretty ace. And none of the Bailey Brothers books combine smuggling *and* piracy.

Chief Clumber had Steve's attention.

"Tell me more," Steve said.

Clumber had recomposed himself. "I'm not supposed to talk about it, Steve."

"Still," said Steve. "Maybe we can help."

"Ha!" said Rick.

"Not *we*," said Dana. "*You*. I don't want to mix it up with pirates."

"Smart boy," said Rick.

"You and I have a history, Chief," said Steve.

"So we do." Clumber picked up a pen and clicked it a couple times. "Maybe you can help. Okay. Here's the situation."

"Oh, come on!" Rick said.

"Quiet, Rick," said Clumber.

Steve pushed his chair's front legs off the ground and began to rock back and forth.

"All right. You've probably seen the container ships off the coast around here," Clumber began.

"Sure," said Steve.

"Well they're mostly bound for Oakland, but it's cheaper to park down here than it is up by the bay. Basically they're down here waiting for the go-ahead from up north to dock."

"Okay," Steve said. Dana looked like he already knew this. Dana read a lot about boats.

"Last night a band of armed . . . well, there's nothing else to call them but pirates, boarded a freighter, overwhelmed the crew, and are right now taking the ship down to Mexico, where they plan to dock at some secret port and off-load all the goods."

"Ace!" said Steve.

Clumber frowned. "No, not 'ace.'"

"Yeah," said Rick. "Definitely not 'ace.'" He shook his head. "That is so not 'ace,' Steve."

"How many pirates are there?" Steve asked.

"It's hard to say. These ships only have four-man crews, but it sounds like these guys weren't taking any chances. One of the sailors guesses there were about twenty of them."

"And how do you know they're going to Mexico?"

"A crewman," Clumber said. He pulled a tape recorder out of his desk. "Those two men in my office earlier were from the FBI and the Coast Guard. They interviewed the crew and, well, listen to this. It's not a very good recording—it's just a copy of the tape. The FBI took the original." He looked peeved.

Clumber pressed play. Two men spoke on the tape. One sounded young, the other old. The recording was muffled at times, and the tape kept clicking.

OLDER MAN: What happened next?

[click click click]

YOUNGER MAN: Well, one of these guys hit me on the back of the head with his gun is what happened next. I went down hard [click] and I just stayed there, you know? [clicking] Like I played 'possum. I figured if I seemed like I was knocked out, these guys wouldn't mess me up anymore. [click click click]

OLDER MAN: And [inaudible over clicking] then?

YOUNGER MAN: Well [click] there were four guys hanging around nearby, and they thought I was out cold, right? So they started talking about how much they were looking forward to getting down to Mexico, all the stuff they were going to get into down there. One of the guys at one point mentioned "the cartel." [click]

OLDER MAN: Do you re-[click click click] they to get into? [click]

YOUNGER MAN: [click] Well . . .

Clumber hit pause. "This clicking is really annoying," he said.

Steve nodded in agreement. At least it wasn't covering up any of the witness's statement. He made some notes in his black book.

"Super annoying," Rick said.

"Anyway, you get the idea," said Clumber. "This kid heard the pirates go over their whole plan. Secret port, cartel, Mexico, everything. Poor guy—apparently it was his first voyage, and he gets coldcocked with a machine gun and thrown in a lifeboat. Of course, the captain is the most upset. Old guy was in tears when he came into the station."

Steve was doing some quick calculations in his head. It would be tough to board a ship secretly and overpower twenty pirates with guns, but he could probably get some backup from the Coast Guard. Plus he'd have Dana. It was doable. Although the best idea was probably to use some sort of subterfuge, like disguising himself as a shipwrecked submariner and aspiring pirate, and tricking the pirates into rescuing him at sea . . .

"But anyway, the ship isn't our problem," Clumber said. "The Coast Guard and the FBI are conducting a heavy search down the coast all the way to Baja."

"Well, how hard can it be to find a big container ship?" Steve asked.

"Harder than you think," said Dana.

"Dana's right," said Clumber. "The ocean's a big place, and these ships go pretty fast. If that freighter hasn't made it to Mexican waters already, it's close. The Coast Guard's only got another couple hours, max. To be honest, I don't think they're going to find the thing."

Steve chewed his lip a bit. "So what's our angle, then?"

"Well, the Feds want our department to be on the lookout around town for any signs of where the gang was holed up—"

"Sea caves," said Steve.

"What?" asked Clumber.

"Smugglers tend to hide out in sea caves."

"No. We're supposed to check out the local hotels, abandoned houses, barns, that sort of thing."

"Oh," said Steve. This case was starting to sound less exciting.

"And," continued Clumber, lowering his voice, "apparently it's common in cases like this for the ringleader of the gang to stay behind and control the situation from land. He may even be here in Ocean Park, monitoring the investigation. We're supposed to be on the lookout for any suspicious out-of-towners. Which, at the start of Ocean Park's tourist season, is a little like finding a needle in a giant stack of needles." Clumber looked pleased with his joke. "Anyway, I get the feeling the Feds are just trying to keep us busy."

"Won't they be surprised," said Rick, "when Rick Elliot delivers the ringleader in cuffs."

Steve closed his notebook, wrapped a rubber band around it, and returned it to his pocket. "I'll make a deal with you, Chief," he said. "If I find this pirate captain, will you arrest these surfers and throw the book at them?"

Clumber mumbled something to himself.

"Come on," said Steve. "You scratch my back, I scratch yours."

"Our back is not exactly itching, Steve," said Rick. "I don't know about your back, but if you need it scratched, then I recommend doing it yourself, 'Detective.' Go buy yourself one of those back scratchers at the detective store and—"

"What are you talking about?" Steve asked.

"Back scratchers," said Rick. "They're a metaphor for—"

"Fine," said Clumber. "You've got a deal."

"Yes!" said Steve.

"But on one condition: You have to get me some

proof these Berserkers stole the surfboards, too. I can't arrest these guys for messing with your bikes."

"Deal," said Steve.

Rick looked disgusted. Steve and Dana rose and headed for the door. "Oh, one more thing," Steve said. "What was on the freighter?"

"Oh," Clumber said. "These ships have a ton of stuff. Furniture, appliances, clothes. But this gang was probably after the Lamborghinis."

CHAPTER XIII

CASELOAD

RICK DROVE STEVE and Dana to the Brixton house.
Dana was spending the night at Steve's.

Steve wrote in his notebook:

CASE NUMBER ONE:
PROVE THE BERSERKERS STOLE SURFBOARDS SO THEY GET PUT IN THE SLAMMER

CASE NUMBER TWO:
FIND THE PIRATE/SMUGGLER RINGLEADER SO CHIEF CLUMBER WILL PUT THE BERSERKERS IN THE SLAMMER

"Rick, could you drive a little smoother?" Steve said. "I'm trying to write."

Rick took a hard turn.

"What are you writing?" Dana asked.

"Just sorting out our mysteries so we can keep them straight. We'll need to stay organized. It can be tough working two cases at once."

Rick scoffed. "Two cases. Big deal. You know how many cases a real professional police officer works at a time? Guess how many cases I've got right now."

"How many?" Dana asked.

"A lot," said Rick. He parked on Driftwood Avenue and threw on the emergency brake.

Before Steve got out of the passenger seat, he casually tore out a page from his notebook.

"Oh, by the way, Rick," Steve said. "Some maniac tried to run us off the road this afternoon. Will you run this plate when you have a chance?"

"No," said Rick.

Steve slammed the door shut. "Too bad," he said to himself.

"What?" Dana asked.

"I'll tell you later."

An hour later Steve was in his bed, and Dana was lying on a bunch of couch cushions he'd arranged on Steve's floor.

"Get some good rest," said Steve. "We start working these cases first thing tomorrow."

CHAPTER XIV

PIRATE SHIPS

AT ELEVEN THIRTY the next morning Steve was in his nightshirt, putting frozen waffles in the toaster.

"You ready for a full day of sleuthing?" Steve asked.

Dana was at the kitchen counter, reading a book about ships.

"Huh?" Dana asked.

"I said are you ready for a full day of sleuthing?"

"I guess," Dana said.

"Do you want one waffle or two?"

"Two."

"That's good. Kevin Bailey says, 'A full belly is a sleuth's best tool.'"

Steve popped the waffles up, flipped them, and pushed the lever down again. If you didn't do that, the waffles got brown on one side and didn't even cook on the other. The toaster just melted the ice and the waffle got wet.

"What happened to Wizards' Worlds?" Steve asked. For a while Dana's girlfriend, whose name was also Dana, had forced him to read a series of books about wizarding, with covers that were all battle-axes and wood nymphs and angry-looking dwarves. It was terrible.

"I finished all of them. *The Infinite Scion* isn't coming out till next year."

"Well there's something to look forward to," Steve said.

The waffles were done. Steve put two more in the toaster. He passed Dana a plate with the syrup and a bottle of squeeze Parkay.

"So here's the plan for today," Steve said. "We have to track down Dromond."

"Dromond?" Dana asked.

"Yeah, that guy in the black Lamborghini who ran us off the road. His license plate says 'Dromond.'"

"Why are we after him?" Dana asked. "Now we're catching a speeder? I thought you weren't taking more than two cases at a time."

Steve filled up each of the little squares in his

waffle with syrup. "I don't care about his reckless driving," Steve said, even though he was actually still furious about what had happened on that bridge. "I'm not sure our friend in the Lamborghini wears a white hat."

Dana looked perplexed. "He wasn't wearing a white hat. He was bald."

Steve sighed. "It's a sleuthing term, Dana. It means he's a baddie. Don't you see?" He pulled out his notebook and jammed his index finger to an open page. "This guy is suspect number one in the piracy case."

MYSTERY: WHO IS THE PIRATE CAPTAIN?

SUSPECT	MOTIVE
1. Dromond	Lamborghinis
2. Rick	Jerk

"Why is Rick on there?" Dana asked.

Steve shrugged. "Tradition."

"I don't know," said Dana. "Doesn't the fact that he's driving a black Lamborghini kind of make him not a suspect?"

"That's insane."

"No. It's smart. Because if I stole a bunch

of Lamborghinis I wouldn't drive around in a Lamborghini."

"You're not thinking like a criminal. Criminals are flashy."

"Okay, but then how did he get the Lamborghini onto the land? And how did he get a custom license plate for it so fast? And wouldn't it be easy to trace the car back to this shipment?"

Steve cut the waffle with his fork. "Don't be ridiculous. I'm not saying that he's driving a stolen Lamborghini. That car's almost definitely clean."

"What *are* you saying?"

"I'm saying this guy loves Lamborghinis!"

Dana frowned. "Seems pretty slim."

"Plus, the guy's got 'Dromond' on his license plate. That's probably his criminal nickname!"

"Dromond?"

"Yeah, I looked it up." Steve slapped a giant dictionary down on the counter. "It's a big old medieval ship."

Dana just chewed.

"Like a *pirate* ship," Steve said.

"Wait, is it just a ship, or is it a pirate ship?"

"Well, it's just a ship, but if pirates were sailing it, then it would be a pirate ship."

Dana nodded skeptically.

"But I'm not even done with the evidence," Steve

said. He went over to the dining room table and brought back another book. This one was called *A Visual Encyclopedia of Piracy*. Torn paper scraps poked up from pages Steve had deemed important.

"Hold on," Steve said. He thumbed through the book and opened it to a drawing of a scowling man with a dark, matted beard. In his right hand was a sword and in his left a black flag that showed a skeleton piercing a red heart with a spear. "Bet you don't know who that is," Steve said.

"It's Blackbeard," said Dana.

"How'd you know?"

Dana shrugged. "The flag."

"Oh," said Steve. "Well. Bet you don't know Blackbeard's real name."

"Nope."

Steve smiled and jabbed his finger at a block of text to the right of Blackbeard's boots.

Name: Blackbeard

Ship: *Queen Anne's Revenge*

Birthplace: England

Real Name: Unknown; various sources give Edward
    Teach, Edward Thatch, or Edward Drummond

Dana flipped the page and studied a diagram of *Queen Anne's Revenge*.

"Hey!" said Steve. "You skipped the clue."

"What clue?" Dana asked.

"His last name was Drummond!"

"Or Thatch."

"Yeah, but the Lamborghini's license plate didn't say 'Thatch.'"

"It didn't say 'Drummond' either. It said 'Dromond.'"

"Well, 'Drummond' is too many letters."

"What about the *o*?" Dana asked. "Drummond" is spelled with a *u*."

"Maybe someone else already had a license plate that said 'Drumond.'"

Dana sighed. "So which is it? The medieval ship, or Blackbeard's name?"

"Maybe it's both," said Steve. "It's like some kind of pirate *double entendre*."

"I don't know. . . ."

"And anyway," said Steve, "the guy was driving very recklessly!"

"Driving crazy doesn't mean you're a pirate captain!" said Dana.

"But it sure doesn't mean you're not," Steve said. He took a long drink of milk to emphasize this last point.

The back door opened. Steve's mom, Carol Brixton, came in from the yard wearing gardening gloves. "Steve," she said, brushing some hair from her face, "there's someone in your doghouse."

"You mean my office."

"Okay."

"What's his name?"

Steve's mom shrugged. "I'm not your secretary, Steve."

"I know," Steve said. Getting a secretary wasn't a bad idea. Maybe Dana would do it.

"Anyway," said Carol, "he says he's got a huge case for you."

Steve and Dana took their waffles with them when they headed out to the yard.

CHAPTER XV

A THIRD MYSTERY

"WOW, I CAN'T believe I'm actually sitting across from the actual Steve Brixton," said the kid in Steve's office. So far, Steve knew this: The kid's name was Brody Owens, and he was a sixth grader at Ocean Park Middle School. He had curly hair that was brownish red, and was big for his age. He was taller than Steve by at least four inches. And he already needed to wear deodorant, although he'd apparently failed to do so this morning.

Steve looked at his watch. They'd been in here talking for nine minutes, and Steve still didn't know why Brody Owens was in his office. "Boy, do I have a case for you," Brody said. It was the fifth time he'd said this today.

"All right," said Steve. "Are you going to tell me or not?"

Brody Owens's forehead was glistening. He lifted up the front of his T-shirt to wipe the sweat off his face. "It's hot in here," he said.

"Uh-huh," said Steve.

"It's too bad your office doesn't have a window," said Brody.

"Well, it does have a door," said Steve. Currently Dana's head was poking through that door. The rest of Dana was still outside—there wasn't much room in the doghouse.

"Yeah, but a window would give you cross-ventilation. It would really cool the place off."

"Noted. What about the case?"

Brody smiled. "Oh boy. Wait till you hear about this. Do I have a case for you."

"I'm all ears," said Steve.

But instead of continuing, Brody looked around the office. "I thought this place would be bigger," he said.

"Sorry to disappoint you," said Steve.

"Oh, oh. I'm not actually that disappointed," Brody replied.

"I wasn't actually that sorry," said Steve. "Look, I've got two cases I'm working on right now, so I don't really have time for—"

"Well, you're about to have three," said Brody. He wore an overachiever's grin. "Are you ready to hear this?"

"Sure am."

Brody pointed his thumb at Dana. "Can he be trusted?"

"Dana's my silent partner in this business," Steve said.

"Not really," said Dana.

"Well, anyway, he's a good chum. I tell him everything."

"Okay," said Brody. "Here we go. Do I have a case for you. It's called . . ." Brody had his hands out like he was holding an invisible beach ball or twelve-foot hoagie. "The Case of the Missing Gym Shorts."

Steve held a pen, but he did not start writing. "Huh?"

"The Case of the Missing Gym Shorts," Brody repeated.

"Okay. What's the problem?"

"Well," said Brody, "Every couple weeks or so, I go to the locker room to change for P.E. I enter the combination on my lock, open the locker door, and my gym shorts are missing!"

"That's it?" said Steve.

"It's happened seven times!" said Brody.

Steve put the pen down and rubbed his forehead.

"Don't you see?" Brody asked. "The lock is still on the locker when I get down there! But my gym shorts are still missing. How are they getting inside? It's a huge mystery!"

"Maybe the thief knows the combination," Steve said. "Have you thought of changing the lock?"

"Yes!"

"And?"

"My dad bought me three new locks. It didn't help!"

"Do you have any enemies?" Steve asked.

"Oh yes," said Brody. "Lots."

Steve wanted to throw his pen out the door.

"But my worst enemy," said Brody, "is probably Bobbie Brethauer. He's always calling me Grody Owens."

"Why?" Dana asked from the doorway.

"Because he says I stink. But I can't help it if I sweat! My dad says all the Owens men are naturally musky. It's in our genes! Oh, he also calls me B. O."

"Look," said Steve. "This Bobbie Brethauer

sounds like a real jerk, but I really can't help you. This isn't really my kind of case."

Brody was crestfallen. "What do you mean?"

"I do jewel heists, smuggling—national security, even. Not penny-ante P.E. pranks."

"But," said Brody, "I already told my dad I was going to hire you. He said I had to figure out who's taking my gym shorts or I couldn't play Nintendo for a month."

"That's not right," Dana said. "It's not your fault somebody's stealing your shorts."

"I know!" said Brody. "But when I told him I was going to hire this private detective who went to my school, he said that was good and he wouldn't take away my privileges."

"I'm sorry," Steve said. "At another time, maybe, but I'm in the middle of some huge stuff."

"But this case could turn out to be huge!" Brody said.

"I seriously doubt that."

"Well, maybe this will change your mind." Brody reached into his backpack. "Moolah."

Brody Owens pulled out a plastic bag full of change and dumped it out on Steve's desk. A couple nickels rolled off onto the floor. "There's fourteen dollars and sixty-three cents there. You can count it.

That ought to be enough to get you started."

"Brody, I charge two hundred dollars a day, plus expenses."

"Oh. That's a lot."

"Yeah."

"Is there like a student discount?"

"Not really."

Brody stood up. He didn't collect his money. "You keep that," he said. "As a deposit."

"Brody," said Steve. "I'm not taking this case."

But the kid was already on his way out the door. "I'll be back," he said.

Steve hoped not. Brody Owens was bad news.

CHAPTER XVI

PUZZLES

"WELL, I THOUGHT it sounded like an interesting case," Dana said as he and Steve walked their bikes into town.

"It was about gym shorts," Steve replied.

"Yeah, but what a great setup. I mean, how is somebody getting to the gym shorts when the locker stays locked?"

"I don't know and I don't want to know."

"I mean, I can only think of two possibilities. One: There's a safecracker in the sixth grade."

"That seems unlikely," Steve said. They paused in front of a pink stucco house to let a car pass through the intersection. "What's two?"

"Well, there are these characters in Wizards' Worlds called the Laughing Assassins, and they can pass through any wall."

"That seems even less likely."

"Exactly. This is an impossible crime!"

"It's just a locked-room mystery."

"A what?"

"A locked-room mystery. It's a kind of mystery that seems impossible, like when some guy goes into a room and locks it, and then the guy gets discovered the next morning, and he's been murdered, only the room is still locked and nobody could have gotten in or out. And it seems like the solution is going to be so crazy and exciting that you read the whole book and then on the last page it turns out that somebody had an extra key or that the killer was hiding in a cabinet the whole time. They always seem impossible, but then there's some trick. They're mostly letdowns."

"Maybe this case will be different," Dana said.

"How?"

"It's a locked-locker mystery." Dana snapped his fingers. "Now, that's a good a name for a case: The Mystery of the Locked Locker."

Steve nodded. "Yeah, that's pretty good." He kicked a pebble down the sidewalk. "Still, it's about gym shorts."

"Brody Owens sure thinks it's a big deal."

"Brody Owens doesn't know what he's talking about." When Steve caught up to the pebble, he kicked it again.

They made a left onto Ocean Park's main drag and dropped their bikes off at the shop. Steve asked the mechanic about the black Lamborghini and was excited to hear that she'd seen the car a few times in the last week.

"Did you see its driver committing any crimes?" Steve asked.

"No," said the mechanic, giving Steve a strange look. He paid a deposit and left the shop.

Steve and Dana then went to the drugstore and each spent four dollars on gum and mints, as they did most Saturdays. Steve and Dana were determined to sample every breath-freshening product in the store, especially the new varieties.

"How's Claire?" Dana asked Steve as they waited in the checkout line.

Claire was Steve's new girlfriend. She lived in another town. He felt weird talking about her. "Fine."

"Have you seen her since Mexico?" They'd started going out after Steve's last case, which had taken them south of the border.

"No. We've talked on the phone a couple times,

but that's it. I mean, she doesn't live that far away, but it's not like we can see each other a lot."

"Yeah."

Products beeped as they were swiped across the scanner.

"Dana," Steve said. "What do you even do when you have a girlfriend?"

Dana shrugged. "I don't know. Dana and I just talk on the phone sometimes, and hold hands and stuff."

"Yeah."

There was more beeping.

"Like, what do you talk about?" Steve asked.

"I don't know. School."

"So like the same stuff we talk about?"

"Yeah, but it's different."

"Right," said Steve. *Beep.* "Different how?"

"Well sometimes I say like . . . sweet stuff, you know?"

"Yeah," said Steve. He didn't know. He had more questions but did not really want to ask them, or hear Dana answer them. Sweet stuff. Steve was grateful when the woman ahead of them paid so he could buy his gum.

"Hey, look," said Dana. He picked up a copy of the *O.P. Outlook* from the newspaper rack. The headline above the fold read PIRATES HIJACK FREIGHTER

OFF CALIFORNIA COAST. Steve scanned the article—
there was no new information—and flipped to page
A15, where the coverage continued. There, next to
a sidebar about the "rumored involvement of local
boy sleuth Steve Brixton," was a small grayscale
photo of Steve.

"Aw, man," said Steve. It was his seventh-grade
school picture—he was wearing his old retainer and
way too much hair gel. Plus he was blinking. "Where
did they get this?"

Steve was furious. Every time the newspaper ran his
picture, it became harder for Steve to maintain a low
profile. The Bailey Brothers were dealing with the con-
sequences of their fame all the time—baddies always
knew when they came to town. As the handbook says,
"For a sleuth, becoming recognizable is almost as bad
as being handcuffed to the steering wheel of a roadster
with no brakes and a puma in the jump seat," which is
exactly what happened to Kevin Bailey in Bailey Brothers #27: *Danger or Bust!* Why did the paper have to
run Steve's photo? And if they did have to run it, why
couldn't they have used a good picture?

Steve was still seething as they left the grocery
store, so it wasn't until Dana elbowed him in the ribs
and pointed that he saw a black Lamborghini parking
down the street.

CHAPTER XVII

TAILING THE SUSPECT

"ALL RIGHT. It's on," said Steve, walking briskly—but naturally, very naturally—down Main Street. Dana was a couple steps behind him. When they were two blocks away, a bald man wearing yellow pants and a golf shirt exited the driver's side of the Lamborghini. The passenger door opened, and a muscle-bound tough in a suit got out.

"Well, would you look at this," Steve said. "Our pirate's got a first mate."

Dana made a noise behind him, and Steve couldn't really tell whether it was a snort or a laugh. More likely it was a laugh—it was a pretty good joke.

The two men were headed to city hall. They walked up a short flight of stairs and disappeared into the building.

Steve stopped short. Dana bumped into Steve's extended arm. "Okay, here's the plan. We've got to be careful. Now that my picture was in the paper, these guys will know who I am, and they'll be on the lookout for me."

"Right," said Dana. "I hadn't thought of that. So we need to disguise ourselves, right?"

"But I didn't pack any disguises," Steve said, "and we don't have time to go to Barney's Costume Planet."

Dana was looking worried. "So what do we do?"

Steve smiled. "Mirrors."

"Mirrors?"

The Bailey Brothers' Detective Handbook has some interesting things to say about mirrors:

As the detective Harris Bailey always tells his sons, "A mystery is a long and crooked road leading to a solution, with danger around every corner." And Harris is right! His statement is true in a figurative sense, but also literally, since goons enjoy hiding around corners, and that's also where baddies usually put traps! Sometimes the Bailey Brothers use mirrors to spot hidden danger. Remember how Shawn used a handheld periscope to see the grizzly lurking in an alley in *The Great Yukon Con*? And mirrors aren't just for corners! Shawn would have never seen the clown tailing him through the haunted house were it not for the shard he carried with him in *The Secret Behind the Fun House Mirror*.

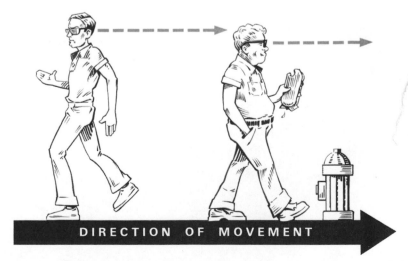

Steve unzipped his backpack and pulled out a pair of sunglasses with extra-wide lenses. "I packed these for you in case we went out surfing again. Eyes in the back of your head. They're mirrored glasses, to protect you from the chimp. If you look off to the sides, you can see whatever is behind you. These are a classic sleuthing tool."

"Cool," Dana said, reaching out for the sunglasses.

"No," said Steve. "Now I need them. They'll help disguise me, but even better, I can follow this guy by walking backward."

"Won't that look obvious?" Dana asked.

"No," said Steve. "Not at all. I'll stop walking whenever he turns around."

"Oh, okay," said Dana. "What am I supposed to do?"

"Well, if you want a mirror, you can run into the drugstore and buy a compact."

"Like a makeup mirror?"

"Yeah. You can hold it out in front of you and see over your shoulder. You can pretend to put makeup on. You know, go undercover as a girl. Ernest Plumly did it in *Misfortune Aboard the Flying Zodiac*."

"What?"

"Your hair is kind of long. He's not going to see your face."

"My hair is not that long."

"Fine, whatever. Really you don't even need a mirror. Your picture isn't in the newspaper."

"Oh, yeah."

"Here they come!" said Steve.

Steve put on his glasses and turned around as the two men left the building. The bald man had a long cardboard tube under his arm and was saying something to his henchman.

Steve followed, walking backward. Dana, walking forward, was at Steve's right.

"Dana, get in front of me or behind me," Steve whispered.

"Why?"

"Because if they turn around, one of us will be facing forward and the other will be backward. That's weird."

"Oh, yeah."

Dana got a few steps behind Steve, which was technically in front of Steve, although Steve couldn't really see him, because he was focusing on where he was walking, which was behind him. It was complicated.

Still, it was pretty ace being able see over your shoulder. At first Steve's steps were awkward, but he was getting the hang of it. People stared as Steve went by, and Dana, following, would wave and smile sheepishly.

The bald man paused and looked up and down the block. Steve halted abruptly and struck up a conversation with Dana.

"Just look at me and pretend that we're talking about the weather," Steve said.

"Okay . . . ," said Dana. "It's . . . sunny today, isn't it?"

"Good," said Steve.

The two men walked across the street.

"Here we go," Steve said, and started walking again.

Steve and Dana crossed after them, in hot if slow-moving pursuit. Steve's eyes were starting to hurt from the walleyed gaze the glasses required. But he pressed on. A little eyestrain never stopped a great sleuth.

Where were they headed? A secret door down some dark alley? A basement tattoo parlor?

The men entered a sandwich shop on the corner of Main and Windward.

"Even villains eat lunch," Steve said, mostly to himself.

Steve and Dana took up a post before a public notice board near the deli. They casually studied the flyers.

"Look at that, somebody lost their Pekingese," Steve said, loud enough so that any passersby would think the boys were two normal young citizens.

Dana got into the spirit. "Violin lessons," he said. "I've always wanted to learn the violin."

"And I've always been interested in the French language," Steve said, tearing off a tab with an instructor's phone number.

"Whoa," Dana said. "Check it out." He pointed at a large white sheet of paper with small black type:

Notice of Public Hearing Concerning

Proposed Development Case Number 20450

Proposed in Ocean Park: A request to allow the development of an approximately 513,047-square-foot boardwalk amusement park and oceanfront entertainment district, including carnival rides, restaurants, sundries, and retail facilities.

PUBLIC HEARING

Date: May 14

Time: 7:00 p.m.

826 Pacific Ave, Ocean Park, CA

DEVELOPER

Hamish L. Omond, Ph.D., Pres.,

Seascapers Construction and Development Co. (SCDC)

"They're going to build an amusement park!" Dana said.

"What?" Steve said. "That's so cool."

"Remember that time my parents took us to Santa Cruz?" Dana said. "I wonder if it'll be like that."

"Yeah, they need, like, an old wooden roller coaster."

"Totally. I wonder if they'll have that thing where you shoot water in a clown's mouth. And Skee-Ball."

"My mom is really good at Skee-Ball," said Steve.

The boys were so involved in their conversation about the amusement park that they almost missed the bald man coming up behind them.

CHAPTER XVIII

HOT PURSUIT

"YES, VERY SUNNY. Sunny and warm," said Steve as the man walked past. The man was alone.

"Where's the goon in the suit?" Steve whispered.

"Probably eating a second sandwich," Dana said.

There was no time to hash out theories. "You wait here in case he comes out," Steve said. "I'll follow our target." Steve jogged in reverse after the bald man.

The man was walking briskly, and Steve struggled to keep up after him. It wasn't easy hustling backward. Steve was almost hit by a car when he was crossing Ozone Avenue, and he lost valuable time by the antique store when he tripped over a small dog. But he managed to keep the pirate's shiny head in his sights.

The sidewalk grew less crowded and the shops fewer. Where was this guy going? He turned onto Wharf Avenue, then made a right on Pacific. They were now walking back toward where they started. The man checked over his shoulder. Steve stared at the back of a diamond-shaped street sign. *SURF BERSERK!* was scrawled on the metal in permanent marker. Well, you could add vandalism of public property to the list of the Berserkers' crimes.

The man went on. So did Steve.

The neighborhood was residential, full of brightly colored houses with ocean views. Narrow alleys named for birds jutted off to Steve's left. Sandpiper, Seagull, Pelican. The man made a right on Petrel. Steve did too, only for him it was a left. The alley was dark. Fences, interrupted every few yards by a garage door, closed in on Steve from either side. Steve watched his footprints appear behind him in the sand. Or was that in front of him?

The pirate was slowing down now, looking off to his right. Steve kept back, and sauntered along with his hands in his pockets. It looked like the pirate was trying to find a particular house—he must be nearing his destination. Steve eyed him carefully, ready for him to enter one of the garages at any moment.

Someone tapped Steve. Reflexively, he looked over his shoulder, even though he could already see behind him and knew there was nobody there. He was tapped again.

Steve's eyes snapped forward. The goon in the suit was inches from his face. While Steve was concentrating on what was happening in the mirrors, this brute had snuck up in front of him. He had one arm wrapped around Dana, and the palm of his hand was clapped over Steve's chum's mouth.

CHAPTER XIX

A BELT IN THE BREADBASKET

"A CHECK TAIL!" Steve said. He shook his head. "I should have known."

"A what?" said the goon in the suit. He voice was deep and raspy.

"A check tail."

"What's that?"

"It's you."

"Huh?"

"A check tail is a guy who follows someone who is following someone else. Don't you know anything about tailing people?" Steve asked.

"I knew enough to catch you, genius," said the thick-necked tough.

Steve had to give him that. He checked the mirrors in his lenses. The pirate in the yellow pants was long gone. "Aw, blast," Steve said.

The man released Dana from his grip and pushed him toward Steve.

"Sorry," Dana said. "He got me right outside the sub shop. He asked me what you were doing, but I wouldn't tell him."

Steve patted his chum on the back.

The goon cracked his knuckles. He had a ring on his right pinkie. The top of a tattoo of the ace of spades peeked out from underneath his collar. He cracked his knuckles again. "Now," said the heavy, "you're going to tell me why you were following my boss."

Steve cracked his knuckles too, only none of them cracked. He whipped off his sunglasses and forced a laugh. "Like you don't know."

The goon looked confused. "I don't know. That's why I asked."

"Take a guess," Steve said.

"No."

"Well, then I'm not going to tell you."

The man's face flushed an ugly red. He took a step toward the boys and looked down at them. "One of you two kids is going to start talking, and fast. Now, who's it gonna be?"

Steve had an idea. "Do you have a quarter?" he asked.

"What?" said the big bruiser.

"Let's flip for it. You seem like a gambling man. I don't want to tell you what we're up to, and my friend *Dwayne Carlton* here"—no need for this felon to know Dana's identity—"doesn't want to tell you, so let's flip a coin. Heads, I talk. Tails, he does."

Dana was baffled. "Well, if one of us is going to tell him, then—"

"No, come on. Let's flip. It'll be more fun."

The tough shrugged. "All I got is a nickel," he said. He pulled out a coin, placed it on his thumb, and launched it in the air. Dana watched the coin rise. The goon watched the coin rise. Steve drove both his fists into the goon's solar plexus.

CHAPTER XX

UP A TREE

THE BAILEY BROTHERS' DETECTIVE HANDBOOK has some excellent advice for sleuths who find themselves pursued by thugs:

Run!

"Run!" Steve said as the big man doubled over. But Dana had already taken off. Steve sprinted after him. He could hear the heavy footfalls of the well-dressed hoodlum echoing behind him.

Up ahead, Dana had already emerged onto the sunny avenue. Steve's chum veered right and disappeared. Dana was fast. Steve was already out of breath.

The footsteps were getting closer. Steve put on his sunglasses. He wasn't happy with what he saw in the mirrors—the goon was gaining on him. At this rate he'd be back in the roughneck's clutches before he made it out of the alley.

Steve had no choice. He hopped a low fence into someone's backyard and scrambled up a tree.

If Steve was lucky, the goon would pass through the yard and never know Steve was in the branches of this oak.

Steve was not lucky. A golden retriever came bounding and barking to the base of the tree.

Steve stared down at the dog's friendly face, its yellow fur fading to white at the tip of its shiny nose.

"Shut up, dog," Steve said.

The dog's pink tongue lolled.

Steve could hear the henchman struggling to climb. The man's ugly mug appeared above the fence. He took one look at the dog, and then at Steve.

Steve sighed and dropped down to the grass. The tough rolled over the fence and into the yard. Steve ran down a narrow passage at the side of the house, past a row of garbage bins. The dog chased him, and so did the goon.

The goon clambered over the fence.

There was a chain-link fence up ahead. The gate was padlocked—Steve could see that already. The fence was too high to climb quickly. He was trapped. The gate clanged when Steve slammed into it. There was no turning back—certain capture lay behind him. Unless, unless . . .

There was a small gap between the gate and a concrete retaining wall. Steve put his right arm through. He sucked in hard and shimmied sideways. The silver fence post pressed against his sternum. The rough wall scraped the backs of Steve's calves. He was almost through. His head felt like it was being squeezed in a vise, and then the pressure was released. Nearly there.

A belt loop on his shorts was stuck on the gate. Only his left leg and arm were still in the yard. Steve rocked his hips back and forth. The goon was forcing the dog out of his way in an effort to reach Steve. The belt loop tore. Steve's leg was through. His pulse thundered.

The goon gripped Steve's left wrist. "Gotcha."

The dog jumped up and licked the goon's face. Steve jerked his arm back.

He was free! Steve ignored the cramp in his side and ran off down the street.

CHAPTER XXI

CLUE-HUNTING

DANA FOUND STEVE sitting beneath a statue outside city hall. The Lamborghini was gone.

"He got away," Steve said.

"What do we do now?" asked Dana.

"Clue-hunting. Come on." Steve led the way into city hall. He walked up to a desk in the middle of a small atrium.

"Excuse me," Steve said to the old lady behind the desk. "I think my dad was in here a little while ago—he was wearing yellow pants and he doesn't have any hair." (The woman smiled.) "Could you tell me where he went?"

"Well, it was to the records office, but—"

Steve made a beeline for a door marked RECORDS.

"But he left twenty minutes ago!" the woman shouted after the boys.

"That's okay," Steve said. "Thanks for your help!"

The room on the other side of the door was divided by a long counter and paneled in dark wood. Three dingy chairs, upholstered in orange, were lined up against one wall. Behind the counter were shelves of books and rows of file cabinets.

"Excuse me," Steve said to a man hunching over some documents on the other side of the counter. The man looked up. He was pale and unfriendly.

"A guy was in here not long ago. Tall, bald, yellow pants," Steve said.

"I can't see people's pants," the man said, indicating the counter.

"Fine. Tall and bald. Remember him?"

"Yes," the man said, squeezing a whole lot of unpleasantness into a very short word.

"What did he want?"

The man made a face like he'd just eaten a sour persimmon. "And why should I tell you?"

The sound of Steve's Velcro wallet opening was loud in the quiet room. Steve waved his official Bailey Brothers detective's license in front of the man's face.

"I'm a private detective, assisting the Ocean Park Police Department in a major investigation."

The man's expression changed. The distaste was still there, but joined by something else: fear. "Yes, I see, all right. Well, he was just picking up some copies of maps he'd requested."

Steve narrowed his eyes. "What kind of maps?"

"Maps of the coastline—the harbor, the bay. A couple nautical maps. Why? Have I done anything wrong? Should I not have given him the maps?"

Steve just shook his head and left.

Outside on the lawn again, Steve was having trouble containing his enthusiasm.

"Can you believe this? Maps! Nautical maps! Wow. Wow."

"So?" Dana said.

"Maps of the harbor? Isn't that exactly what you would want . . . if you were planning on hijacking a ship?"

Dana shook his head. "I don't get it. They already stole the ship."

Steve grinned. "Don't you see what this means, Dana? The pirates are going to strike again!"

CHAPTER XXII

BRODY'S BACK

WHEN THEY GOT BACK to Steve's backyard office, Brody Owens was waiting for them.

The big kid was fanning himself with today's paper. "Great article in here, Steve. You must be really pleased."

Steve shrugged. "What's going on, Brody?"

"I'm steaming in here, that's what's going on!" Brody said. "I feel like a lobster." He chuckled.

"Uh-huh," said Steve. He sat on his desk and flipped on the lamp.

"Seriously, Steve, it's really stuffy in here."

"I feel fine," Steve said. "Can I help you with something?"

"Yeah, my case!" Brody said. "Doi! Have you forgotten already? I thought you were supposed to be a crack detective!"

"I remember your case, Brody," Steve said.

"I know, I know," said Brody. "I'm just joshing. I came to give you this." He pulled out a small plastic bag and put it on the table. Steve picked it up and put it under the light.

"What is it?" Dana asked. This time Steve's chum had managed to squeeze into the office and was crouching in the corner.

"It's a penny," said Steve. "Look, I wasn't going to take the case for fourteen dollars and sixty-three cents, and I'm not going to take it for fourteen sixty-four."

Brody just laughed. "That's not just a penny, Mr. Detective Man. That's my mint-condition 1914-D penny, and it's worth six hundred sixty-eight dollars and seventy-five cents."

Dana whistled. Steve didn't know what to say.

"That right there is three full days of detective work," Brody said. "If you can't crack the case before then, well, maybe you aren't the detective we all think you are."

Steve exhaled and shook his head. "Brody, it's not the money. I don't want this case."

"I thought you were supposed to be a crack detective."

But Brody had already risen and was ducking through the door. "Happy sleuthing!" he said, and trudged across Steve's backyard.

"Hi, Carol!" Brody said. "Lovely evening, isn't it?"

"It sure is, Brody!" said Carol Brixton. "Do you need a soda for the walk home?"

Steve's mom was giving out his sodas? This was unbelievable.

"He's right about one thing," Dana said, sitting in the chair Brody had just vacated. "This place could use a window."

CHAPTER XXIII

SWELLS

"How am I supposed to put a window in the office?" Steve was saying to, or really shouting at, Dana as they walked into town on Sunday morning. "Keep in mind it used to be a doghouse. I think it's looking pretty good."

"Well, I think a window would really open the place up. Right now it feels a little . . . claustrophobic."

"Claustrophobic? Claustrophobic? That's just . . ." Steve trailed off.

"You wouldn't even need to put in an actual window. I was thinking: What if you just put a picture of an outdoor scene on the wall, and frame it so it looks like a window?"

"That's the dumbest thing I've ever heard," Steve said.

"Why?"

"Because. What about when it's nighttime? When you look out this window, there'll still be a day scene."

"Oh, yeah," said Dana.

"What would be smart," Steve said, "is to get a double-sided frame, and put one picture with a day scene, and one picture with a night scene, and then you flip it over when the sun goes down."

"That is really smart," Dana said.

Before they picked up their bikes, they stopped by the drugstore.

"Where are your double-sided picture frames?" Steve asked a teenager in a red apron.

"We don't have those," she said. "Is that even something that exists?"

In the end Steve ended up buying two picture frames and a hot-glue gun, plus two posters to cut up and frame. The drugstore didn't have a great poster selection, but Steve picked out one that showed some lambs grazing in a pasture, which he thought would relax him in the middle of a tough case, and one of a city at night, where the lights from cars were just blurry lines all over the streets. The nighttime poster was gritty and fully ace.

They picked up their bikes, retrieved Steve's surfboard from its hiding place by the road, and pedaled to Swells. The same clerk was sitting behind the register, watching another surf video. A high-school girl was sitting on the counter. She was wearing cut-off shorts and an old white T-shirt over a blue bikini top, and she looked bored.

The clerk seemed excited to see Steve and Dana.

"Lizzie, these are the groms I was telling you about!"

Lizzie looked up mildly. "Oh, yeah? You guys are crazy."

"Glad you guys aren't dead," said the clerk. "I was worried about you."

"Did you guys paddle out at Point Panic?" Lizzie asked.

"Yeah," said Steve. He slapped the wetsuits down on the counter. "We caught some good rides, too, until those Berserkers starting messing with us."

"Hold on. You did not stand up," the clerk said.

"We did," said Steve. "We got cozy in some barrels."

The clerk shook his head. "If you say so, dude. What about the Berserkers?"

Steve told them about the confrontation on the water. Even Lizzie seemed impressed.

"Tremor is not to be messed with," the clerk said. "You're lucky you still have ten fingers."

"I was more worried about the chimp," Steve said.

"Oh, you mean Eric?" Lizzie said. "That's Tremor's brother. He's sweet, once you get to know him."

"The chimp's name is Eric?" Steve asked.

"How do you know Eric?" the clerk asked.

Lizzie shrugged. "I used to hang around with those guys."

"You did?" asked the clerk.

"Yeah, they threw these great parties on Clothesline Beach every full moon. I went with Sarah. It was really fun."

"But you don't go anymore, right?" asked the clerk.

"No. Calm down. Anyway the parties aren't even at Clothesline anymore—they moved them to Mímulo. I'm not driving all the way down there."

"Not even to see Eric?"

"Stop."

"Okay, I have a question: Why does that guy wear a chimp mask?" Steve asked.

"I don't know," Lizzie said. "I think he's just kind of weird. But he should take it off: He's kind of cute."

"You've seen him without the mask?" Dana said.

"You think Eric is cute?" asked the clerk.

"I think we should keep calling him the chimp," said Steve.

"Look, guys," said the clerk. "Eric, or the chimp, or whatever, is not sweet. That whole gang is merciless."

"But they still have my client's board," Steve said, "and one of your boards too."

The clerk waved it off. "That board was just an old beater—it was waterlogged and totally dinged up. We probably should have gotten rid of it already. If it will keep you out of the ocean, I'll give you the deposit back. Seriously, bro, it's not worth your life."

"Thanks," said Steve. That was nice of the guy. But the Berserkers still had Danimal's board, probably in the back of that leopard-spotted truck. And even though Steve was closing in on the pirate captain, he still needed proof that the Berserkers were thieves if Clumber was going to arrest them. Steve had been hired to do a job, and he would see it through to its finish.

"We'll take your advice," Steve said. "I guess I'll return this board, then. But could we rent the wetsuits for the week? I think we might try some bodysurfing down at Cowry Cove."

"Sure thing, big guy. That sounds like it would be just your speed."

Steve watched the television while the clerk rang

him up. Surfers sped down the faces of massive waves the size of buildings. The video cut from ride to ride, backed by pounding drums. Steve was mesmerized. A woman took off down a mountain of water, her hair a flash of white.

Dana leaned forward. "Is that Ms. Bundt?"

Steve squinted. The footage was grainy, and the woman moved fast, but his chum was right: That was Ocean Park's librarian.

"Who?" asked the clerk, looking up distractedly.

"Oh, we thought we recognized that last surfer."

"Doubt it. Nobody knows who she is. She came out of nowhere five years ago and charged Todos Santos, and was never heard from again. They call her *la Gata*."

Steve just shook his head and paid for the suits.

A bell rang as they walked out the door.

"I'm excited to go bodysurfing," Dana said as he unlocked his bike.

Steve was stuffing his wetsuit in his backpack. "We're not going bodysurfing," he said.

"Then why—"

"Full moon's Wednesday. We're going to a beach party."

CHAPTER XXIV

THE NOOSE TIGHTENS

THE BOYS BIKED back along the ocean. Rocky hillsides gave way to great glass houses, and soon they sped by a sign that said WELCOME TO OCEAN PARK. There were lots of streetlights on this section of Pacific Avenue, so the boys cut through the marina parking lot. They weaved around couples carrying picnic baskets and trucks towing motorboats. Their shocks thudded when their bikes took the speed bumps.

"Well, lookie here," Steve said, squeezing his brakes hard.

Dana skidded and stopped a few feet ahead. "What?"

The Lamborghini was turning into the parking lot.

Steve and Dana watched from behind a garbage can as the black car pulled into a space. Two spaces, really: The pirate captain parked right on the line between two slots like a total jerk. The man and his goon emerged, carrying brown bags.

"Wonder what's in the bags?" Dana said.

"Probably weapons," said Steve, "or groceries."

The men strolled down a dock, unmoored a small launch, and started its engine.

"Now, where are they going in that tiny thing?" Steve wondered.

"There." Dana pointed to a yacht bobbing next to a buoy past the entrance of the marina. Even from a distance, Steve could see that the boat was huge. Its masts poked skyward, but the sails were down. Steve tried to whistle, but it came out as more of a squeak.

"That's a nice yacht," Dana said. "Really nice. Probably seventy, eighty feet long."

"Why's it parked all the way out there?" Steve asked.

"Too big for the marina," Dana said.

"Nice and private out there too." Steve made some notes in his book. "How fast can a ship like that go?"

"Fast," Dana said.

Steve smiled. "The noose tightens," he said.

CHAPTER XXV

AN ANGRY MAN

LATER THAT AFTERNOON, Steve hung the window up in his office.

"It's a little crooked," Dana said, looking up from his book. "Higher on the left. Now lower. Too low."

Steve ground his molars together. "I think maybe the wall isn't even," he said.

"Well you can't have a crooked window," said Dana.

"I know that; it's just—"

Someone knocked above the door.

"Come in," said Steve.

Their guest was a big man with curly red hair. To

accommodate him, Steve had to throw both chairs and his desk on the lawn. Only the lamp remained, sitting on the floor. Steve, Dana, and the man were packed shoulder to shoulder in the office. Steve guessed the man's identity before he'd even introduced himself.

"Tom Owens," said the man. "I'm Brody's dad. Which one of you twerps ripped off my son?"

"Ripped off?" said Steve.

"You got a hearing problem, or was I just not loud enough?" The man was being plenty loud enough. "Who is Steve?"

"Steve is Steve," said Dana, pointing. He was so close that his index finger poked Steve.

The man gave Steve a once-over. "You're the detective, huh? Brody tells me you made him give you his penny. My father gave me that penny, and I gave it to Brody. You know how much that thing is worth?"

"Six-hundred sixty-eight dollars and seventy-five cents."

Tom Owens was taken aback. "Yeah."

"Look, if you want the penny—"

"What's a kid like you going to do with that kind of money, anyway? I could hire a real detective for that kind of moolah."

Steve drove his fingernails into his palms. "I am a real detective," he said.

"Yeah?" said Tom Owens. "Then why's your name painted on a dog bone above the door to your office?"

"Because," said Steve, "I dig up the bone of truth."

"Hey, that's pretty good," said Dana.

"I'm not talking to you," said Tom Owens.

"Look," said Steve, "like I was saying, if you want the penny back, you can have it."

"Of course I want it back. That's why I came over here, isn't it?"

"Fine," said Steve. "Then please turn around."

"What?"

"Turn around."

"There's no room to turn around."

"Then just cover your *eyes*."

Tom Owens put his hands over his face.

Steve pulled up a loose floorboard and took out an old *Guinness Book of World Records*. He opened it up to reveal a secret compartment that held, among other things, the 1914-D penny. After returning the book to its hiding place, Steve said, "Okay."

Tom Owens snatched the coin out of Steve's hand. "Thanks," he said.

"Don't mention it," said Steve.

Tom Owens's face softened. "You're still going to help Brody find his gym shorts, aren't you?"

"I never agreed to find them in the first place," said Steve.

"Then why'd you take his money?"

"I didn't."

"Is this guy a weasel or what?" Tom Owens's last question was directed at Dana, who answered with a cold stare.

The digital watch on Tom Owens's massive wrist started beeping. "Well, boys, I've got to scram. Time to transfer the laundry. I swear, if I'm not buying Brody a new pair of shorts, I'm washing an old pair. Now, I used to sweat a lot too when I was Brody's age—the Owens men sweat, and that's the way it is—but I don't remember my dad washing my gym clothes every weekend."

Tom Owens backed out of the office and disappeared across the yard.

"Well," said Dana, stretching, "looks like you'll just have to work the gym-shorts case pro bono."

CHAPTER XXVI

SWEET STUFF

MONDAY WAS a school holiday, so Steve woke up late and ate a leisurely breakfast. When he was finished, he put his dishes in the sink. Then he walked into the living room and picked up the phone.

He listened to the dial tone.

Then he hung up the phone again.

The Bailey Brothers' Detective Handbook says, "When you're interrogating a suspect, plan out the whole conversation to make sure the baddie doesn't get the upper hand."

Steve wasn't planning to interrogate a suspect— he was calling Claire Marriner—but the handbook didn't really have any advice about talking to girls, and Steve wanted this conversation to go well. So it was probably better to plan it out anyway.

Sweet stuff. Dana had said it was important to say sweet stuff. Steve had been trying to think of some sweet stuff ever since, and last night he'd come up with something good. The conversation would go down like this:

STEVE BRIXTON: Hi, Claire.

CLAIRE MARRINER: Hi, Steve! How's sleuthing?

STEVE BRIXTON: Oh, you know, business as usual.

CLAIRE MARRINER: Ha ha. Cool. So how was your week?

STEVE BRIXTON: Oh, it was pretty good. We had P.E. on Thursday and we played baseball.

CLAIRE MARRINER: What position did you play?

STEVE BRIXTON: Outfield. And I played way better than I usually do.

CLAIRE MARRINER: Really? Why do you think you played so well?

STEVE BRIXTON: Because I was thinking of you.

CLAIRE MARRINER: That's really sweet!

STEVE BRIXTON: It's true.

CLAIRE MARRINER: And it's such a nice compliment. Thank you, Steve.

STEVE BRIXTON: You're welcome.

CLAIRE MARRINER: Bye!

STEVE BRIXTON: Bye!

The bit about playing well wasn't true. Steve wasn't very good at baseball. But he had been thinking of Claire during P.E., and it sounded even better if thinking of her made him field better. Steve dialed Claire's number.

"Hello?" A man's gruff voice was on the other end of the line. Cy Marriner, Claire's uncle.

"Hi, is Claire there?"

"Who's this?"

"Um, Steve."

"Steve who?"

"Steve Brixton."

"You should always say your first and last name when you call someone, Steven."

"Just Steve."

"What?"

"Never mind."

The man grunted, set down the phone, and called Claire. Steve tried to regroup.

"Hello?" It was Claire.

"Hey, Claire. It's Steve Brixton."

"Hi, Steve! How's it going?"

"Oh, you know, business as usual."

"What?"

"Sleuthing."

"Oh. Right. Well, it's good to hear from you."

"You too! Well, I mean to hear you. Not to hear from you. Because I called."

"Yeah."

Steve was pacing around the sofa. He had to get this conversation back on track.

"Well, I've missed you," said Claire.

"My week went pretty well," said Steve.

"Oh. Okay."

"Really well."

"That's great."

Steve picked up a couch cushion with his free hand and started swinging it around. "We had P.E. this week," he said.

"Oh. Don't you have P.E. every week?"

"Yeah."

"Cool. We do too."

"We're doing baseball in P.E. right now."

"Nice. We're doing soccer."

"I was in the outfield. And I did really well."

"That's great."

"Like, really well."

"Okay . . ."

"I was catching so many pop-ups. And stuff."

"Right."

"Want to know why?"

"Sure . . ."

"Because I was thinking of you." Steve hurled the cushion at the love seat across the coffee table.

"Oh. Well. That's nice."

"Yeah."

Nobody spoke for what seemed like a while. Steve could hear music in the background at Claire's house.

"Well, I've got to go," Steve said. "I'm on a case."

"Okay. Bye."

"Bye."

Steve hung up the phone and dropped it on the sofa.

That had gone pretty well.

Actually, it had not gone well at all.

Maybe he should call back.

But then again, he was already late for a stakeout.

CHAPTER XXVII

SURVEILLANCE

EVERYTHING STEVE KNEW about stakeouts he learned from *The Bailey Brothers' Detective Handbook:*

The Bailey Brothers love a good stakeout, also known as "fixed surveillance" or a "plant"—but not the kind that grows in soil! A stakeout is called a plant because the observant sleuth stays "planted" in one place. It's best to choose a place that's well hidden, like inside an empty apartment, atop a high building, or behind a large plant—the kind that actually does grow in soil! A sleuth on a stakeout always remembers to bring a telescope and plenty of snacks!

There wasn't really anywhere to hide in the marina—he didn't know anyone who owned a boat. Steve sat on a metal bench. He didn't own a telescope, either, but that was all right. He figured he probably would have looked conspicuous sitting on that bench, peering into a telescope in broad daylight.

Steve did bring along his mom's point-and-shoot camera, which had a 5X zoom lens. But when Steve looked at the yacht at full zoom, it appeared smaller than it did to the naked eye. So Steve sat and watched.

He thought about Claire Marriner. The conversation had not gone as planned. Still, maybe she had liked the stuff about P.E. class. Although it really didn't seem like she had. How had everything gone wrong? He'd had the sweet stuff all planned out, but then Cy had answered the phone, and that had ruined everything right away.

Steve needed to focus. On a stakeout, everything could go crazy in a split second.

Within an hour he had eaten all his snacks (two

pudding cups, three packets of fruit snacks, and a tangerine).

After an hour and a half, he took out his notebook and began to write.

TO DO THIS WEEK

*Foil second hijacking attempt

*Prove bald guy is pirate captain

*Gather evidence of Berserkers' theft at full-

moon party

*Submit new photo to local newspapers

Between those tasks and any homework that got assigned, it was going to be a busy week.

By the end of the day, he'd filled up another page in his notebook.

SURVEILLANCE NOTES

2 p.m.: Nothing has happened.

2:53: Still nothing.

Steve was on a stakeout!

3:34: A crazy lady yelled at me that this was her

bench. I told her it was a free country.

4:15: There is a man here with an actual parrot!

I bet he is cool.

4:48: Parrot guy just talked to me for 27

minutes. He was weird but not really cool.

5:25: I wonder if they are even on that dumb boat.

5:28: Why didn't I ask Claire how her week was?

5:35: Just realized I should have looked to see

if the Lamborghini was in the parking lot.

It was.

5:43: I really should have asked her about her week.

5:45: A light went on on the yacht!

6:03: Nothing has happened.

By half past six it was too dark to see. Steve walked across the street to a convenience store and bought a postcard of an old station wagon with a bunch of surfboards strapped to the roof. He flipped the card over, addressed it to Claire, and affixed the postage stamp he kept in his wallet in case he was kidnapped and needed to send the authorities his location.

Steve bit the end of his pen, then wrote, *Hi, Claire. How was your week?*

Steve dropped it in the mailbox on his way home.

CHAPTER XXVIII

A SINISTER WARNING

THAT NIGHT STEVE had the dream again, the one he'd been having every night since Friday. He was soaked and cold and lying on his back in the sand. It was dawn, or dusk, and the sky was gray and misty. He could hear the ocean but couldn't see it. The chimp was standing over him, holding a knife. The knife was the same knife he'd had in the water, only in the dream the knife was much bigger. The chimp was laughing underneath his mask. Steve couldn't see the chimp's face, but he could tell from the muffled noises he was making and the way his chest rose and fell beneath his black wetsuit.

Steve opened his mouth to challenge the chimp, but no words came out.

The chimp threw down the knife. It stuck, handle up, in the wet sand.

And then slowly, almost gracefully, the chimp reached up and removed his mask.

This was where the dream got weird. The first night, beneath the mask had been the head of a monster. The second night, it had been the bald pirate captain. Last night, it had been Steve's mom. Tonight, when the chimp tore off the rubber mask, Steve was looking up at the sneering face of MacArthur Bart.

Steve awoke to the sound of breaking glass. He checked his alarm clock—it was almost four a.m. Dogs were barking in the night. He heard footsteps in the yard. Steve went to his window, cupped his hands around his eyes, and looked out. No one was there. But he was sure he'd heard something. He took his flashlight from his bedside table, grabbed a pair of flip-flops, and tiptoed into the hall. He could hear his mom breathing regularly in her bedroom. Once he'd picked his way down the stairs and eased the back door open, he put on the flip-flops and walked across the lawn, arching his soles so the sandals neither flipped nor flopped. The dew was cold on his toes and made the shoes' rubber pads slippery.

Steve flipped on his flashlight. Everything in the backyard was in order. His bike was still there. His mom's gardening equipment was all accounted for. An old, flat basketball was still in the corner. Steve didn't know why he checked on the basketball.

Steve crossed to his office and shone the beam through the doorway. The ground was covered with shattered glass. His window lay lamb-side up, surrounded by shards. Who would do this? Steve trained his beam on a red brick lying on the floorboards. A piece of paper was attached to the brick with a rubber band. Steve got his pink dishwashing gloves and put them on—he didn't want to mess up any fingerprints. Holding the flashlight in his mouth, Steve removed the piece of paper and unfolded it. There was a message neatly written in blue ink:

BRIXTON: DROP THE CASE
IF YOU WANT TO SEE YOUR
THIRTEENTH BIRTHDAY

CHAPTER XXIX

STRANGE CURRENTS

ON TUESDAY, after first period, Steve showed Dana the warning.

"Whoa," said Dana. "Freaky."

"Yeah," said Steve, putting some books in his locker. "But which case is it talking about? The Berserkers? Or the piracy case?"

"Or the gym shorts," Dana added.

"I didn't take the gym-shorts case," Steve said.

"Yeah, but does the gym-shorts robber know that?" Dana said. "I think Brody's been telling everyone you're on the job. Five *sixth graders* have already come up to me asking about it."

"I really don't think this is about the gym shorts," Steve said.

"Yeah, but you can't rule it out," said Dana. "A good sleuth rules out only the impossible theories. The best sleuths refuse to rule out even those."

Steve gaped. "How do you know that?"

"Yesterday I skimmed *The Bailey Brothers' Detective Handbook* a little."

"What? Why? I've been trying to get you to read the handbook forever."

"I was just thinking about the gym-shorts case, and I thought it might help."

"Why are you—"

Steve was interrupted by the approach of Brody Owens.

"Guys," he said. He looked pale and worried. "It's happened again. My gym shorts are missing."

CHAPTER XXX

AN ODD DEVELOPMENT

AFTER SCHOOL, Steve and Dana walked home down the road that ran along the ocean.

"Mind if we check something out?" Steve said.

They took a detour and ended up in the marina. Things looked pretty much like they had yesterday— even the man with the parrot was back—but there was one important difference: The yacht was gone.

"What do you think it means?" Dana asked as Steve stared out to sea.

"I don't know," said Steve. "But I don't like it."

"Do you think . . . ," said Dana.

"What?" said Steve.

"Well, do you think it's a coincidence that the yacht has vanished on the same day Brody's gym shorts were stolen?"

Steve turned to his chum. "Are you serious?"

"Yeah."

"There's no way these cases are linked," said Steve.

"Well, it's just that I looked at a couple Bailey Brothers books yesterday, and it seems like whenever there are two mysteries, they always come together."

"Don't tell me what happens in the Bailey Brothers. I know all about the Bailey Brothers. I already have two mysteries. And they're already coming together: If I prove the bald man is the pirate captain, then Chief Clumber will arrest the Berserkers. The end. The gym-shorts case is not going to tie into anything, because I didn't take the case."

"Fine," Dana said. As Steve stalked off, he heard his friend mutter, "We'll see."

CHAPTER XXXI

INTERROGATION

A KID WAS WAITING in Steve's office after school on Wednesday. He was short and wiry, but Steve could tell he was an athlete just by the way he sat.

"Who are you?" Steve asked, squeezing past the kid and standing behind his desk.

"This is Bobbie Brethauer," Dana said.

Bobbie Brethauer nodded.

Steve took his seat. "Okay," he said. "Why are you here?"

"I hear I'm the top suspect in the Owens case," said Bobbie.

Steve rubbed his right temple with two fingers. "Where'd you hear that?"

"He told me," Bobbie said, nodding toward Dana.
Steve glared at Dana, but Dana was watching
Bobbie.

"You're not a suspect," Steve said.

"Good," said Bobbie. "Because I didn't do it."

"And how do we know that?" Dana asked.

"Not my style," said Bobbie. "I mean, I don't like
Grody Owens." He paused to see if Steve would
laugh. He didn't. "That kid's a little crybaby. But I
just give him wedgies and stuff. Wet willies. Funny
stuff. Stuff that makes everybody laugh."

"Uh-huh," said Steve. Bobbie Brethauer was hard
to like.

"I mean, if I took his gym shorts, he'd know it.
I'd fly them up the flagpole or stick them on his
head or something." Bobbie chortled. "Yeah, I'd
stick them on his head. But really, I wouldn't touch
those things. They're disgusting. That guy sweats
like a pig."

"Pigs don't sweat," Steve and Dana said at the
same time. Steve wanted to jinx his chum but that
would have seemed unprofessional.

"Anyway, I just wanted to tell you you're after the
wrong guy," Bobbie said.

"I'm not after anybody," said Steve.

"Whatever," said Bobbie. "Good luck with the
case."

When Bobbie Brethauer was gone, Dana asked, "Do you believe him?"

Steve sighed. "Yes."

"Me too," Dana said. "I don't like him, but I believe him. A guy like that wants credit for his pranks." Dana looked up at the ceiling. "I wonder if we have to rethink the motive here."

"Look . . . ," began Steve.

Carol Brixton knocked on the wall of the office. "Steve, phone." She thrust the cordless through the doorway. "It's Chief Clumber."

Steve grabbed the handset. "What is it, Chief?"

The connection was bad this far from the house, and there was static on the line.

"Steve." Clumber sounded far away. "They got another freighter last night."

CHAPTER XXXII

PHANTOM FREIGHTER

IT WAS ALMOST just like last time—the pirates struck at night and threw the crew overboard in a lifeboat. The castaways hadn't been found till this morning. The ship was probably halfway to Mexico by now.

"Why didn't you tell me earlier?" Steve asked.

"You were at school," said Chief Clumber.

Steve was pacing around his office. "What was on the boat this time?" Steve asked. "Lamborghinis?"

"No," said Chief Clumber. "This time it was mostly toys from China."

"Toys?"

"Yeah, stuffed animals, Hula-Hoops, Frisbees . . ."

"I get it," Steve said.

"This is a real black eye for the department."

"I'm working on it, Chief," said Steve.

"Okay." Clumber sounded morose. "Steve?"

"Yeah?"

"Thanks."

Steve hung up the phone and went over to his map. Lamborghinis he could understand. But toys? What kind of money could these pirates get for smuggling teddy bears? He put another yellow pin off the coast of California, south of the pin that marked the place the first ship had been taken.

"Dana," Steve said. "Why are there eight yellow pins on our school?"

He already knew the answer before Dana said it. "Gym shorts."

Dana joined Steve at the map.

"Gym shorts go missing, ship goes missing," Dana said.

Steve ignored him. "Come on. I want to check on something."

They rode their bikes down to the marina. But Steve saw it before he'd even turned into the parking lot: The yacht was back.

Steve shook his head. "Things are really heating up," he said. "Tonight's a big night."

"I know," said Dana. "I feel like we're about to crack this gym-shorts case wide open."

"Not the gym shorts," Steve said. "It's Wednesday. Tonight we raid the Berserkers' party."

CHAPTER XXXIII

FROGMEN

THAT NIGHT STEVE and Dana snuck out of their houses and rode south on Highway 1. The boys got in the water at Bandon Beach and, wearing wetsuits, swam for the sandy shores beneath Point Panic. The full moon shone bluish white overhead, and left a whitish blue reflection in the ocean. The water was freezing.

It was a lot harder to swim two miles than to walk them. After fifteen minutes Steve was out of breath, and his arms felt heavy. He rotated between strokes—breaststroke, freestyle, and doggy paddle—to try to give muscle groups a break. But soon enough he was cycling through strokes so quickly that it really didn't matter: Steve was beat. He was glad that Dana seemed to be tired too.

They let the current take them along the coast. As they drifted around a gentle bend, Steve saw a distant speck of orange down the shore. Fire. That was their destination. The flames grew brighter and bigger, and before long Steve could hear music: acoustic guitars and wild drumming. There were shouts and the sounds of bottles breaking on rocks.

The prospect of serious sleuthing renewed Steve Brixton. He swam silently on, Dana close behind him. To his left he heard the sound of big waves breaking around Mímulo Point. The party was directly to his right.

They let the waves carry them onto the beach and then crawled on their bellies across the sand. Hidden behind a boulder twenty feet from the fire, Steve and Dana observed the ruckus. There were a couple dozen people at the party, guys and girls, laughing and stumbling and dancing. Some people played instruments. One lay flat on his back and shouted things that made the whole group laugh. Steve recognized most of the faces from the week before. Tremor sat by the fire, nodding his head to the rhythm of the bongos. The chimp was throwing his knife at a large piece of driftwood while someone who looked

There were wild shapes and bloodcurdling cries.

a lot like Lizzie watched. The green-haired surfer was boxing with another kid—from here it was hard to tell whether the fight was serious. Surfboards stuck straight out of the sand like spears.

"What's the plan?" Dana asked.

"The plan," Steve said, "is to sneak over there while they're distracted and see if we can find the key to the truck. Then we find Danimal's board."

"I think they'll notice us," said Dana.

"Yeah, of course they would if we tried right now," said Steve. "We have to wait for our moment."

Just then, Tremor rose. Steve saw for the first time that the surfer wore a fur cape over his bare shoulders. The big man gestured to the chimp. They exchanged a few sentences, and Tremor gestured to the rock where Steve and Dana hid. The chimp nodded.

"Oh no," said Dana.

The two surfers were coming right for them.

CHAPTER XXXIV

BERSERKERGANG

STEVE CLENCHED his fists and prepared to fight, but Tremor and the chimp stopped in front of the rock.

"Tell the guys we're paddling out for another moonlight session tomorrow night. There's a big swell coming in, and we're going to ride it."

The chimp spoke next: "Are we taking down the boardwalker?"

Dana's forehead furrowed. Steve, horror-struck, mouthed, *Danimal*.

It was clear from Dana's expression that he had trouble reading Steve's lips.

"You know it," said Tremor. Steve could hear the smile on the man's lips.

The boys listened to the slapping palms of an

elaborate handshake and heard the two Berserkers trudge back to the party.

"What was that all about?" Dana asked.

"I don't know, but I think they're out to get Danimal."

"What do you mean?"

"'Boardwalker.' Remember the guy in the surf shop told us you can only walk around on longboards? They're going to take him down tomorrow night."

"Oh man," Dana said.

"We have to warn him," said Steve. Dana agreed.

When Tremor returned to the fire, he addressed the gathering. "Berserkers!" he shouted.

The guitars faded away. The crowd grew silent.

"Feel the fury!"

The beat of the drums had become driving and primal. Shirtless Berserkers, clad only in board shorts, danced and stomped around the bonfire. The chimp threw the driftwood into the flames—the fire sparked and sizzled.

The girls stood at the edges of the light—some watched, most talked. A few people were leaving, making their way up the trail to the road.

The drums grew louder and faster. The surfers circled the flames. Their teeth chattered like dogs biting at fleas. Lit by the fire, their faces loomed large and seemed to change color: red and black and green and orange. The drums beat on. The surfers howled and shrieked. They leapt and shook. The bonfire was all frenzied motion and terrible noise. The screams reached a crescendo, then stopped.

The Berserkers picked up boards and charged, bare-chested, into the Pacific.

"That was weird," said Steve.

"Those guys must be freezing." Dana and Steve watched the surfers paddling out in the moonlit waters. The girls who'd remained made their way to the water's edge to better see the Berserkers surf.

"Now's our chance," said Steve, bolting out from behind the boulder.

He and Dana scoured the area around the bonfire, looking under cans and inside jeans pockets.

"Here!" Dana said. He held up a gray hooded sweatshirt and shook it. Inside its kangaroo pocket, keys jangled.

Steve rushed over as Dana pulled out a silver ring with a Viking-helmet key chain.

"Let's go!" Steve said. They scrambled up the palisade. There were more cars parked on the highway's shoulder tonight, but the leopard-spotted truck was closest to the trail. The moon was so bright Steve could read SURF BERSERK, even from a few yards away.

Only one key looked like it would work in a truck. Dana slid it into the lock on the driver-side door. There was a pop. Steve tried the handle. The door opened.

CHAPTER XXXV

RECOVERING THE DINGUS

THE BACK OF the ice cream truck smelled foul, and Steve couldn't see a thing.

"Why didn't you bring a flashlight?" Dana asked.

"Because we made an amphibious assault," said Steve. "You can't put a flashlight in the ocean."

"You could with a waterproof flashlight," said Dana.

"Yeah, but I don't own a waterproof flashlight," said Steve. "Do you?"

"No."

Steve didn't like it, but they were going to have to turn on the interior lights and just hope nobody walked by. All the Berserkers were out on the water, so it should be safe. Steve slid back into the driver's seat and felt along the dash until he felt a switch. He flipped it.

A tinny jingle blared from many speakers: "Turkey in the Straw," a.k.a. the ice cream song.

"What are you doing?" Dana shouted.

Steve flipped the switch off. "Sorry."

He flipped another switch. The truck blasted another tune. "The Entertainer," a.k.a. the other ice cream song.

"Steve!"

"Sorry." He found the light switch.

"Look at that," said Dana.

A large rubber shark fin sat on top of a pile of scuba equipment. An ugly device that looked like an old bear trap lay open nearby.

Steve picked up the fin. It was slimy and flopped in his hand. "These are the guys who were faking the shark attacks, too," he said. He added impersonating a great white to the Berserkers' rap sheet.

He tossed the fin back on the floor of the van. "Let's keep moving. There," he said. He pointed to the big board bag he'd seen last Friday.

Dana unzipped it.

Danimal's surfboard was inside.

The board was beautiful. Twice as tall as Steve and

bright red, with a long wooden strip running down the middle. A thumb-shaped single fin protruded from the underside, and the nose arched up slightly in a lovely curve.

"We got it!" Steve said. "We got the proof!"

He picked up the board. It was heavy.

"Grab the other side of this," Steve said. "We can bring it back to Danimal, and then send the cops out here once we solve the other case."

"But if the board's gone, won't the Berserkers know we're onto them?"

Dana had a point. But they couldn't just leave the board here. Could they?

Steve thought it over. But before he could make up his mind, the front door to the ice cream truck slid open.

Steve and Dana froze, illuminated by the dome light overhead.

The chimp and Lizzie stared at them.

"Hey, guys," said Lizzie.

"Aloha," said Steve.

The chimp didn't say a word.

CHAPTER XXXVI

BUSTIN' SURFBOARDS

THE CHIMP HAULED them back down the trail and held them on the beach until the rest of the Berserkers came in from their session. Steve and Dana sat on a log while the chimp threw his knife in the sand.

By the time Tremor returned, the bonfire had burned down to embers.

"All right," Tremor said. The party had clearly broken up. The Berserkers were all arrayed behind Tremor, and everyone else had left.

"I am giving you one chance," Tremor said, "to tell me the truth. Why do you two keep snooping around here?"

Steve looked Tremor in the eye. (It was hard not to focus on those horns.) "Okay," he said. "Fine. Here's the truth. My friend and I are professional surfers from Hawaii and we want to—"

Tremor bellowed.

Steve winced.

The green-haired surfer clucked his tongue at Steve, and the metal piercing made ugly clicks inside his mouth.

"The truth," Tremor said.

Steve noticed that the chimp had his knife in hand.

"I'm a private investigator," Steve said.

"I know that," said Tremor. "I saw your picture in the paper. Now, why are you hanging around?"

"I was hired by a guy named Danimal to get his board back."

Tremor's eyes widened. And then he started laughing. "You want that old board?"

"Actually two boards," said Dana. "I think you guys stole my board too."

"We junked that one, big guy," Tremor said. "Thing was barely seaworthy."

Steve could tell Dana was angry. He wanted to tell his chum not to worry, that they'd have their revenge soon. "Anyway," said Steve, "Just give us Danimal's board and we'll get going."

"And what if I don't want to give you the board back?"

"You have to. We caught you red-handed."

Tremor waved his hand dismissively. "So what? Your friend Danimal was trespassing. This is our wave."

Steve stood. "You don't own the ocean!"

"You know how many surfers there were in 1959?"

"Why do I care?" Steve said.

"Do you know how many surfers there were in 1959?" Tremor repeated.

"No."

"Five thousand. In the whole world. Know how many there are today?"

Steve sighed. "No."

"Over a million. It used to be a crowded lineup was nine of your best buddies. Now there's a gaggle of kooks overrunning every decent break in California. Kooks ruin waves. Someone has to stop them."

"The Berserkers to the rescue!" Steve said. He wanted to spit for emphasis, but his mouth was dry.

"Someone has to protect the waves. Who's gonna do it? The police protect houses and cars and stuff, right? Well, I don't have a house. I don't have a car. I just care about waves. But the police, they don't care about waves. They should, but they don't.

When someone doesn't know what they're doing out there, it's dangerous for everybody. When a wave is crowded, people get hurt. So who will protect us from the kooks? Who will protect the kooks from themselves? We will. We are our own police." Tremor raised his eyebrows at Steve. "And really, isn't that exactly what you are?"

"What?" Steve said.

"You're a detective, right? People hire you for cases the police don't want, or cases they don't want the police involved in. You operate on the edges, the places police won't go. Or can't go. You decide what the law is, what's right and what's wrong, and then you enforce it yourself. You and me, bro, we're the same."

"No." Steve said. "You're wrong. No."

Tremor was amused. "How are you different?"

"I go after the truth. I do what's right."

"What *you* think is right. I do what *I* think is right. I think it's right that this wave gets the riders it deserves."

"I don't steal people's boards."

"You wouldn't steal if it helped you solve a case? If it helped you get the truth?"

Steve mentally reviewed a list of things he'd stolen on the job—a hotel key card, a police car, a truck, a bottle of lavender bubble bath. But he'd given them all back, except for the bubble bath, and those were basically free when you stayed at the hotel, only Steve hadn't been staying at the hotel, but still, he'd needed it for self-defense. Steve decided not to answer Tremor's question.

But there was a difference, and Steve knew it. It wasn't the same, what he did—*what the Bailey Brothers did*—and what these Berserkers were doing. The line might be blurry, but Steve was on the right side of that line. He knew it, even if he couldn't explain it.

Tremor continued. "We're outcasts. We live outside the borders." Tremor gestured toward the sea. "This country was built by people like us—loners and outsiders, pioneers who went their own way and made their own rules. The surfer and the private eye: We're the two great American icons of rugged individualism, bro."

"What about cowboys?" Dana said.

"What?" said Tremor.

"Cowboys. They're icons of rugged individualism, or whatever."

Tremor turned his hands palms up and shook his head. "All right. Cowboys are in the top three."

"Well, I think they're probably number one. Cowboys are way more iconic than surfers or private eyes."

Steve shook his head. "Definitely not more than private eyes."

"Or surfers," Tremor said.

"Yeah, you guys *would* say that. You're biased. I'm not. I'm not a cowboy, or a surfer, or a detective."

"You kind of are a detective," Steve said.

Dana shook his head. "Nope."

"Come on, you're Mr. Gym Shorts these days."

"That's just a little dabbling," Dana said. "I'm definitely not—"

"Enough," said Tremor. "You guys really want that board back?"

Steve looked at Tremor like he was an idiot. "Yeah. Duh."

"Eric, go get that Mal. Bring a nice coffin bag, too."

The chimp ran up to the truck. Steve pressed the button to illuminate the face of his calculator watch. It was almost one.

The chimp returned with Danimal's board under his arm. He carried a nice cushioned board bag, too, which was unexpectedly kind: It had handles, and would definitely make the trip back to Ocean Park easier. Although the bag looked a tad too small.

Tremor hefted Danimal's board easily and looked it up and down. "It's a real beauty," he said. "I'll be sorry to see it go."

Tremor took a few long strides over to the boulder Steve and Dana had been hiding behind earlier. He gave his head a single shake. The muscles in his neck tensed. Then he lifted the board like a giant ax and swung it against the rock.

The crack was terrible, and rang against the cliffs.

The board was not quite snapped in two. The top half was bent back like a badly broken arm. Tremor finished the job by bringing the board down over his knee.

He walked up to Steve with a piece of the board in each hand.

"Here's your buddy's board," he said, flinging the pieces on the ground. He spat. "Eric, get these two heroes out of my sight."

CHAPTER XXXVII

IN THE BAG

THE CHIMP PUT the two halves of Danimal's board in the coffin bag, then ordered Steve and Dana to get in the bag too.

Steve slumped. It was humiliating, but the guy had a knife. He walked over to the bag and lay down. Dana got in next to him.

"This is bad," said Steve's chum.

Steve heard the zipper. The last thing he saw before the darkness was the chimp's smile.

They were lifted and carried roughly up the trail.

"You should have made them walk up the cliff and then put them in the bag," said a voice that

Steve and Dana were sealed in the coffin bag.

Steve recognized as the green-haired surfer's.

"They can hear you," said the chimp.

"So what?" said Green.

"So don't second-guess me," said the chimp.

"It's not too late. We can still let them get out and walk."

"Yeah, that would look great."

"I don't care how it looks. They're heavy."

"Shut up. Shut up, shut up."

The rest of the trip up the trail was silent. The boys were thrown in the back of the ice cream truck, and the engine started. As the car rolled forward, "Turkey in the Straw" began playing. They drove for about ten minutes, south (Steve was keeping track of the turns). Then the car parked, a door slid open, and they were roughly dropped on uneven ground. The ice cream truck roared back to life, and its tune faded into the night.

After a minute of silence Dana asked, "Think the coast is clear?"

Steve forced the zipper open from the inside. The two boys rose from the coffin bag. They were by the side of the highway. The only sound was the ocean slamming against the shore.

"That didn't go very well," Dana said.

Steve stared into the bag. So that's how this case

ended—with a board broken in two. He thought of MacArthur Bart, out free in the world. Sometimes cases didn't finish well. Sometimes a mystery was like an itch you wished you'd never scratched. That was one thing the Bailey Brothers books didn't prepare you for.

He and Dana each grabbed a piece of Danimal's board and started walking toward Ocean Park.

CHAPTER XXXVIII

BREAK

DANIMAL LOOKED like he might cry.

It was four thirty on Thursday afternoon. The board lay in two pieces on the floor of Steve's office.

"They'll pay," Steve said. "I promise they'll pay. I made a deal with Chief Clumber, and if I can just wrap up this other case, he promised he'll throw these guys in jail."

Danimal nodded.

"It's not over yet, Danimal," Steve said.

"That was a great board," Danimal said. He stood up to go.

"Danimal, wait," Steve said. "I have a question. What's a moonlight session?"

Danimal looked dazed. "Night surfing. When the moon is bright, you can catch some waves without everybody else crowding the lineup. It's great."

"Well, Danimal, don't go out tonight. I'm pretty sure the Berserkers aren't finished with you. Last night they were talking about taking you down."

"Why? What did I do to these guys? I just wanted to surf my favorite spot."

"These guys are serious about that wave," Steve said.

Danimal nodded. He gathered up the pieces of his board and left.

Steve took out his notebook and crossed out

CASE NUMBER ONE:
PROVE THE BERSERKERS STOLE SURFBOARDS SO THEY GET PUT IN THE SLAMMER

"Well, that was hard," Steve said. Still, he had the evidence needed to put the Berserkers behind bars.

Now he had to solve case number two: the smuggling case. But all he had was a pile of clues pointing toward that yacht—nothing that would hold up in court. Steve needed to hand the pirate captain to Chief Clumber in cuffs.

"Look at these names," Dana said. "It'll cheer you up."

It was a grid with words and numbers. A list of last names ran down the side.

Appel
Arquillos
Bennet
Chau
Franklin
Galante
Garcia
Hom
Johnson
✦ ✦**Lowenstein** ✦ ✦
Martin
Panoriñgan
Ramos
Viera

"Notice anything?" Dana asked.

"I noticed that you highlighted 'Lowenstein' and put lots of stars around it."

"Yeah, but do you know why?"

"No idea."

Dana grinned. "This is the roster Coach P. uses to keep track of the mile times for the sixth-grade boys, a.k.a. our suspect list in the gym-shorts case."

"Your suspect list," said Steve.

"And there is suspect number one," said Dana. "Aaron Lowenstein."

"I don't get it," Steve said.

"Well, I got to thinking, if nobody is *pranking* Brody, then why would someone take his gym shorts? And then it came to me. Obviously: to have them for himself."

"Eight pairs?"

"Maybe the kid is forgetful," Dana said. "Or maybe he likes wearing stolen goods."

"Hmm."

"Anyway, there was just one thing I couldn't figure out." Dana pulled his gym shorts out of his backpack. "We all write our last names on our shorts." He pointed to a yellow bar, below the letters OPMS in which he'd written "Villalon" in permanent marker. "That way nobody accidentally takes our shorts—or steals them."

"Right."

"It's a pretty good theft deterrent. Unless . . ."— Dana paused for effect—"your last name is Lowenstein! Think about it—his name contains Brody's last name. All Aaron would have to do is add an *L* to the beginning and *T-E-I-N* to the end! It's the perfect crime."

"That is not the perfect crime," Steve said.

"Why isn't it the perfect crime?" Dana asked.

It was a pretty good crime.

"Look, Dana, I don't have time to explain the ins and outs of criminology to you right now, okay? My case is at a dead end."

"Whoa," Dana said. "Fine."

Steve knocked some papers off his desk. He stormed out of his office and headed out toward downtown.

CHAPTER XXXIX

ICE CREAM

STEVE WALKED the streets of Ocean Park till it was dark. Eventually he wound up at Rocky's Ice Creamery, looking for a mint chip sundae and a little good luck. The Bailey Brothers always ate ice cream when they were stumped, and Rocky's was where Steve had cracked his first case. He took a seat at the counter and placed his order.

The sundae was delicious. Steve hadn't had mint chip since the time he'd badly bitten his tongue on the job. Man, that had hurt. Steve wondered whether that Berserker's tongue piercing was painful. Probably, at least at first. Steve decided he would never do that to his own tongue, not even if it was an excuse to eat mint chip ice cream every day. It looked stupid, for one thing. Plus it kept making that annoying clicking sound.

Something clicked in Steve's brain.

But before he could sort it out, Rocky came over, wiping the counter down with a damp cloth.

"Hey, Steve," said Rocky. He was an old guy with long gray hair gathered up in a ponytail. He looked agitated tonight. "You see this business?"

Rocky produced a copy of the public notice Steve had read a couple days before, the one announcing the proposed amusement park down by the beach.

"Yeah," said Steve. He licked some warm chocolate syrup off his spoon. "Sounds cool."

Rocky snorted. "Cool? Cool. Yeah, you would think that. You're a kid. You don't have to think about a business."

"Hey, I own a business," Steve said.

"Yeah, well, you don't have to feed a family."

"That's true," Steve said. "What's the matter, though? Doesn't your family like roller coasters?"

"Roller coasters. You would think about the roller coasters, and nothing else. Look at this." He underlined a sentence on the flyer with his index finger. "Will include 'restaurants, sundries, and retail facilities.' Sundries. Know what 'sundries' means?"

"No."

"Well, neither do I, really, but it means there's gonna be an ice cream stand."

"Oh."

"How would you feel if another private eye moved into Ocean Park?"

Steve thought about that. He was pretty sure that he'd be better at solving mysteries than anyone else in California. Still, in the Bailey Brothers books, sometimes the sloppy sleuth Oliver Champ elbowed in on the boys' cases, and that always fouled everything up. Maybe Rocky had a point.

"This developer comes in and builds a beach boardwalk, everybody's gonna get their ice cream from him. Trust me—that's how it goes. This guy built another one of these boardwalks down south, and it put a store like mine right out of business."

"But your ice cream is good, Rocky."

"Yeah, that don't matter. These big-money developers know how to put the squeeze on guys like me. But I'll tell you one thing: A bunch of us businesses are going to this hearing, and we're going to block this thing. This guy thinks he can sail up from L.A. on his fancy boat and steamroll Ocean Park? No way."

Steve's pulse quickened. He bit his thumbnail. Rocky kept looking at the paper in his hands.

"Hamish L. Omond," said Rocky. "And he's one of these fellas who makes you call him doctor, even though he's not a *real* doctor—he's got his Ph.D. in something like 'hospitality management.' Sounds made up. But I'm marching right into that meeting and I'm going to say, 'With respect, *Mister* Omond. Oh, I'm sorry, *Doctor* Omond.'"

Steve stood up. He reached in his pocket and slapped a ten-dollar bill on the table, then ran out of the shop.

CHAPTER XL

REENLISTING A CHUM

STEVE JAMMED his finger on Dana's doorbell over and over. Finally his chum came to the door.

"Chum," said Steve.

"Don't call me—"

"We don't have time for that now," Steve said.

"All right," Dana said. "But, Steve . . ."

Steve didn't have time for this. "What?"

"I know how you're feeling."

"What?"

"I know how you're feeling. You know, stumped."

"What are you talking about?"

"I staked out Aaron Lowenstein's house this

afternoon. Turns out the kid is tiny. There's no way he could wear Brody's shorts. Now it looks like all the cases are at dead ends."

"No," Steve said, almost breathless. "I'm not stumped anymore. Look, we need to work tonight. It's time to go catch the pirates."

"What?"

"I don't have time to explain." He thrust Dana's wetsuit through the door. "You need to pretend to go to bed right now, then sneak out. Meet me at the marina. Wear this."

"But it's only seven forty-five."

"I know. But we're not supposed to be out after eight, so if we want to work tonight, we have to go to bed and then sneak out."

"But what if I don't really want to work tonight?" Dana said. "I didn't get much sleep last night."

"But you just said it was too early to go to bed!"

"Okay, so maybe I don't want to get kidnapped two nights in a row."

"Last night we did not get kidnapped. We got stuffed in a coffin bag and dropped off by the highway."

Dana looked uncertain.

"Look," Steve said. "What if you're right, and the gym shorts are tied into this pirate case?"

"I'm in," said Dana.

"Good. Tell your parents you're going to bed, wait a half hour, then head out."

"All right," said Dana. "I'll tell them I'm not feeling well."

"Don't do that," said Steve. "If you say you're sick, they'll check on you. Just say you're tired."

"Right."

"Be at the marina as soon as you can."

CHAPTER XLI

INTO THE WATER

IT WAS PAST ten thirty when Steve reached the marina. Dana was already there, sitting on a bench.

"What took you so long?" Dana asked as Steve locked up his bike.

"Mom and Rick were watching a movie."

"I've been here for over an hour."

"Well, your bedroom is on the first floor. It's easier to sneak out of."

"Still."

Steve looked out to the buoy. The yacht was moored there, and lights were on aboard the boat. Good. There was still time to stop them.

"Come on," Steve said, and headed for a slipway that sloped into the water.

"We're swimming?" Dana asked.

"Why do you think I told you to wear your wetsuit?" Steve said.

"You're not supposed to swim in the marina."

Steve just walked down the slipway. He braced himself for the frigid shock to come. When he was deep enough, he dunked his head beneath the surface—it was better to get it all over with at once.

It took a little over an hour for Steve and Dana to swim out through the marina's entrance. Twenty minutes later they were treading water a few yards from the yacht, close enough to read the boat's name, although Steve already knew it.

They had to hurry.

"Dana, how can we get on this boat?"

"There should be a ladder at the stern," Dana said.

"Great," said Steve. "Where is the stern?"

"The back," said Dana.

"Right."

They cut silent strokes through the black waters and made their way astern. There was a ladder, just like Dana said. It was long and silver, like the one in the deep end of the community swimming pool, and it almost sparkled in the moonlight.

"I'll go first," Steve said, gripping the rails with either hand.

It was a long way up. The rungs of the ladder were rough on Steve's bare feet. Near the top, he noticed a small black Zodiac boat strapped to a platform that jutted out from the yacht. "That's the lifeboat," Dana said.

"Good to know," said Steve.

Steve reached the top of the ladder and climbed over a flexible metal guardrail to reach the deck. Dana was right behind him.

"Okay, where do you think the bald man and that goon would be?" Steve asked.

"Probably asleep."

"They're not asleep—the lights were on when we were swimming up here."

"Okay, then probably the saloon."

"The saloon?"

"That's what you call the, like, living room on a yacht."

"A saloon?"

"Come on, follow me," Dana said.

They made their way along the deck until they came to a white door. Windows high on the wall shone yellow, and music was playing within.

"I think they're in there," Dana said. "What's the plan?"

Steve flung the door open.

CHAPTER XLII

THE VILLAINS REVEALED

THE BALD MAN and the goon were surprised to see the boys, and that gave Steve a few moments to check out the room. The place was all blond wood, white leather, and elegant curves. Deep-pile taupe carpeting covered the floor. Every tabletop and counter was heavily lacquered, and their surfaces gleamed in the light from what seemed like hundreds of recessed fixtures in the ceiling. There was a Jacuzzi in the corner. Smooth jazz played from speakers Steve couldn't see.

The goon was grilling fish and vegetables on a large, semicircular stainless-steel grill. The bald man was wearing a captain's hat, and he sat on a bar stool at a counter that ran along the grill's perimeter. He held a fork in his hand, a piece of uneaten bok choy still speared on its tines.

"You again," said the goon, who, instead of wearing a suit, was clad in all white. His sleeves were rolled up, revealing two thick forearms. "What are you—"

Before Steve could talk, Dana was pointing a finger at the pair.

"All right, gentlemen. The jig is up!" Dana said. "We know all about your operation—Steve figured it out. Piracy *and* smuggling *and* who knows what else."

"Dana," said Steve.

"Well, it's all over now. And when Steve is finished with you, I have a couple questions of my own."

"Dana."

The fish was burning on the grill. The goon clumsily tried to flip the fillets with a spatula, but their undersides were blackened. The grill sizzled, and a bright blue flame erupted. The bald man flinched while the goon beat the stove with a dish towel.

"You know," Dana said. "You two make a sorry couple of pirates."

The bald man was flummoxed. "We're not pirates."

"Yeah, technically you are," said Dana.

"No, we're not," said the goon.

"They're not," said Steve.

"What?" said Dana.

"They aren't pirates."

"I thought we were coming to stop the pirates."

"We are, but they're not the pirates."

"Why didn't you tell me that earlier?"

"There wasn't enough time."

"It would have taken like one minute."

"I would have taken longer than a minute."

"Still."

"Look, we didn't have time to waste."

"Call the harbor police, Mickey," the bald man told the heavy.

"Go ahead, call the police," Steve said. He'd rather they didn't call, though. Steve wanted to deliver the culprits to the cops himself—it was the detective's prerogative. "But you're probably wasting your time. At any moment, this ship is going to be hijacked by pirate smugglers. But I have a plan to stop them, Dr. Omond."

"How do you know my name?" the bald man asked.

"Yeah, how do you know his name?" said Dana.

"It's on his license plate," Steve said. "*D-R-O-M-O-N-D*. He's Dr. Hamish L. Omond, the developer who wants to build the beach boardwalk."

"That's true," said Dr. Omond.

"You really should have explained this to me," Dana said.

"Listen, Dr. Omond," said Steve. "I'm sure you've heard that pirates have been stealing ships off the coast of Ocean Park. Your yacht's next unless we act now."

"Who are you?" Dr. Omond said.

"I'm Steve Brixton, the private detective," said Steve.

"Oh, and I'm Dana," said Dana.

"I did see something about this kid in the papers," said Mickey. "Although you look different from your photo."

"Yeah, I know," Steve said. "Listen, we have to move."

"Mickey, radio the police," Dr. Omond said.

Mickey walked over to the receiver.

"But—" said Steve.

"What's your plan?" Dr. Omond asked skeptically.

"Okay," said Steve. "First I need you guys to play opossum—"

"Captain," said Mickey. "The radio's dead."

"What?" said Dr. Omond.

"I don't understand. It was working earlier."

"Dana and I will hide—"

"Oh, now you'll explain things to me, now that you need my help."

"All right—here's the explanation. Dr. Omond is 'Dromond.' He was getting maps from city hall because he wants to build a beach boardwalk. His ship is called the *Boardwalker*. That's what the Berserkers were talking about last night. When they say a moonlight session, they mean hijacking a boat. The green-haired surfer was the sailor on the tape in Clumber's office, although his hair probably wasn't green when he was on the freighter. He was an inside man. The clicking on the tape was the clicking of his tongue ring—that's why it never covered up the sailor's words. The Berserkers are going to hijack this yacht."

"See, that didn't take too long."

"Okay, here's the plan—"

The door to the saloon swung open. Five men holding machine guns and wearing stockings over their faces poured into the room.

The saloon was overrun by gun-toting pirates.

CHAPTER XLIII

CAPTURED!

IF ONLY EVERYBODY had stopped talking and listened to Steve, there might have been time for his plan. Now they were sunk.

"Hey, Tremor," Steve said to the masked man at the front of the pack.

The man paused, then peeled off the stocking. "Guess I don't need this." Tremor looked weird without his helmet. "Look, guys, it's the heroes!"

The five other men peeled off their masks. Steve recognized them from the beach.

"How'd you know it was us?" Tremor asked.

"Are you joking me? All right. Dr. Omond is

'Dromond.' He was getting maps from city hall because he wants to build—"

"Never mind. We don't have time for this."

Steve sighed.

"Let's get sailing," Tremor said. His four companions hustled out the door. "Send Eric and Tremblay to guard these guys once we're under way."

"Where are you taking us?" asked Dr. Omond.

"Mexico," Steve said. He was already formulating a plan for fighting his way out of the gang's secret Mexican headquarters.

Tremor laughed. "We're not going to Mexico. We're going surfing."

CHAPTER XLIV

BERSERK

"SURFING," SAID STEVE. "But the sailor said . . . oh."

"There you go," said Tremor. "Now you get it, bro. That's why we planted Tremblay on that freighter. So he could steer the cops in the wrong direction. He made it sound like there were more of us than there were, like we were a real sophisticated operation with ties to Mexico. We don't have any connections to any cartels, bro. We aren't smugglers. Those ships are about ten miles off the coast."

The yacht started moving.

"What good are Lamborghinis if they're floating in the middle of the ocean?" Dana asked.

"I don't care about Lamborghinis," Tremor said. "And those container ships aren't floating. We sank them."

"What?" Unbelievable. These guys were nuts. "Why?"

"We made a wave."

"You made a wave?" Steve said. "You can't make a wave."

"I think he means figuratively," Dana said.

"No, I mean literally," said Tremor.

"You can't literally make a wave," Dana said.

"Sure you can," said Tremor. "Waves break when swells of the right size hit floors of the right depth. We found a shelf off the coast that's just right for some monster waves—it was just about a hundred feet too shallow. So we hijacked some freighters, dynamited them in the middle of the night, and boom, we made a wave. Two waves, technically." He brought his index fingers together and slowly spread them out to each shoulder. "We used two ships, so this wave breaks both ways, a thousand feet in either direction. My brother rides regular foot, but I ride goofy."

"You guys dynamited two freighters just so you could make a break?"

"Our own break," said Tremor. "No kooks. No

outsiders. This is a giant wave only Berserkers can ride. The ultimate Mysto spot."

"How giant?" Steve asked.

"Giant," said Tremor, "Should be thirty-five, forty feet in the right conditions. We've got a big swell coming tonight. It'll be the first time Berserk goes off."

"Berserk?" Steve asked.

"What did you think we'd name the break?" Tremor said. He gave himself Viking horns with his pinkies. "Surf Berserk."

"So why are you stealing the *Boardwalker*?" Dr. Omond asked weakly.

"We're moving out to the ocean, Doc," said Tremor. "If we're gonna live out there most of the year, we might as well do it on a nice boat. I'm tired of sleeping in an ice cream truck. What is that?" Tremor pointed to the grill. "A teppanyaki barbecue?"

"Yes," said Dr. Omond.

"You gotta have a teppanyaki barbecue," Tremor said.

There was a knock at the door.

Tremor opened it.

The chimp and the green-haired surfer were standing on the deck.

"Eric. Tremblay. You guys guard the door. We'll

rotate watches until we figure out what we're doing with them."

"Why don't we just drown 'em?" Tremblay said.

Tremor rubbed his chin. "Maybe. But not yet," he said. "Not here."

The leader of the Berserkers exited the saloon, and the door slammed shut behind him.

CHAPTER XLV

MYSTO

THEY HEARD BERSERK before they saw it.

They sailed for an hour under a nearly full moon before the break was audible. It started as a far-off susurration and became a stormy rustle, and then, as the seas grew rough, the sound of Berserk was the only sound: the pounding, rushing, hissing sound of a giant wave.

The din would erupt every five minutes, rage for a few minutes more, and then subside.

Steve peered out a window, but it was too dark to make out the break.

The mood in the saloon was low. Nobody spoke.

CHAPTER XLVI

GETAWAY!

DANA WENT FIRST, shimmying a bit to get up the vertical part of the vent. Then Mickey boosted Steve up into the hood, and Steve groped around in the blackness till he felt Dana's hand. His chum pulled him up, and they started to crawl. Their elbows tucked tightly beneath their ribs, the boys wriggled forward. The metal was greasy, and Steve sweated in his wetsuit. He tried not to breathe—the shaft smelled like fish.

"I feel a breeze up ahead," Dana whispered.

They inched on.

"There's some sort of covering blocking the end of this thing," said Dana. Steve heard his chum struggling against metal. There was a soft clang, and Steve felt a blast of cold, salty air.

He dropped a few feet onto the yacht's deck. Coming out of the vent face-first, it was impossible to make a graceful landing—Steve landed on his belly.

They had emerged amidships. Berserk was crashing nearby. Dana was crouching next to Steve, staring out to sea. Steve looked out over the rails. They were behind the wave, but even from this angle Steve could tell Berserk was huge. It jacked up out of the sea, and from the back the wave looked as tall as Steve's house and as long as his block. He couldn't imagine what it was like being on the other side, riding the thing. He could just make out the shapes of surfers bobbing up and down on their boards, and sometimes he could hear their wild hooting.

Dana tapped Steve on the shoulder. He pointed left, then led the way.

As the boys crept down the gangway, the yacht pitched and yawed. Steve had to grab the guardrail to keep his balance. The rail was just a thin metal cable, anchored to the deck every four feet by a flimsy perpendicular stanchion. It had a lot of give, and Steve swayed and slipped.

Steve could feel every beat of his heart. The boys were almost to the stern—just about twenty feet to go—when someone shouted, "Hey!"

Steve turned and looked over his shoulder.

It was the chimp.

CHAPTER XLVII

BRAWL AMIDSHIPS

THE CHIMP was standing behind them with a long, narrow surfboard under his arm. He dropped the board and reached behind him. When his hand came forward, it was holding the diving knife.

Without thinking, Steve charged the man, screaming. The chimp hesitated. Even the mask seemed to wear a stunned expression. Then the chimp swung, his knife flashing, but Steve knew it was coming. He dropped to the deck, safe from the blade, and grabbed the board. The masked goon stabbed downward, but Steve was already up and running back toward Dana. The board's leash reached its full length and then grew taut. The man's right leg, attached by the ankle to the board in Steve's arms, flew forward. The chimp slipped, and for a moment seemed to hang in the air before crashing downward. There was a crack as his head hit the deck.

The chimp did not get up.

"I think I kayoed him," Steve said.

Dana had come up behind him. "Come on, let's go."

"Hold on," Steve said. "I have to see something."

He cautiously stepped toward the body of the man before him. Steve kept a careful eye on the rise and fall of the chimp's chest, ready to bolt at the sign of any sudden movement. He bent down until he was inches from the man's face, then slipped his index finger beneath the rubber edge of the mask.

Slowly Steve pulled the mask back.

The face underneath was freckled and pale. The chimp looked a lot like Tremor, but younger, with a weaker chin. He had brown hair and a slightly upturned nose. It was an unremarkable face. Steve stood up. He wished he'd never taken off the mask.

"Come on!" Dana said.

But when they turned toward the stern, they saw Tremblay coming toward them.

There was no time to think. Steve unfastened the leash from the chimp's ankle and threw the board over the guardrail.

"Jump!" Steve said.

They did.

CHAPTER XLVIII

CAUGHT INSIDE

THE BOARD WAS yellow and purple and long enough for both of them. Steve was up near the front, which was pointy, and Dana was at the back, which was also pointy. Steve looked over his shoulder. Tremblay was leaning over the guardrail, shouting, but Steve doubted the other Berserkers could hear him. He couldn't seem to make up his mind about whether to jump in after them or stay on the ship.

He jumped.

"Paddle!" Steve shouted. "Right! Left! Right! Left!"

Steve and Dana coordinated their strokes, paddling frantically forward. They were leaving

Tremblay behind them, but heading toward the pack of Berserkers.

"Turn! Turn!"

It was harder to coordinate the turning. The board nose wobbled left, then right, and the choppy waters made precision impossible.

Tremblay was gaining on them.

"Just go!" Steve said. "Right! Left! Right!"

They picked up speed.

"Steve!" Dana shouted.

Steve glanced over his shoulder at his chum.

"Look!"

Steve looked.

The ocean was rising up.

"Left! Left! Left!"

A swell was coming in.

Unless they could make it up its face, the first wave of the set would come down right on of top them.

The nose of their board pointed directly at the swell.

"Now go! Left! Right! Left! Right!"

Steve dug his arms deep beneath the surface of the water as the set came rolling in.

What started as a bump turned into a bolus and then, off to their left, became a wedge.

"Go-go-go-go-go-go!"

Berserk was starting to break. They were paddling uphill now, and the wave was drawing them upward, upward. It felt like being caught up in the vein of some tremendous beast.

Steve looked off to his left again.

A man in a metal helmet was dropping down the face, his right leg pushed out defiantly toward the tip of his board.

Steve's arms worked quickly even as Tremor's ride unfolded slowly before him. Tremor slid down the face of the massive wave, cut a wide turn at the bottom, and ended up right in the barrel, framed by a cascading wall of whitewater. The barrel collapsed, letting out a massive spray of whitewater that seemed to propel Tremor toward Steve and Dana's board. He carved a path up the face of the wave coming right at them. Tremor's mouth was open and his eyes were wild, but Steve could hear no scream over the sound of the water.

Their board was almost vertical now, almost over the lip. But Tremor was hurtling toward them. Teeth. There were sharks' teeth in the nose of that board, and the nose was aimed right at Steve's head. Tremor sped up the face of the wave, getting closer and closer, until Steve was sure he could see the sharks' teeth gleam in the moonlight.

This was bad.

Surf Berserk!

"Bail!" Steve shouted. He rolled to the right, and with his legs swept Dana off with him. But Steve kept his hands on the rails of the board, and tipped it toward him like a shield. The impact of Tremor's collision reverberated through the surfboard as they passed over the crest. The last thing Steve saw before they dropped down the wave's back side was Tremor flying forward, over the falls.

CHAPTER XLIX

IMPACT ZONE

STEVE RIGHTED the board. There was a huge gash in it now, but it was in one piece. He and Dana got back on and started paddling right away. The next wave was even bigger than the last, but they were in a better position. They paddled up a thirty-foot face and dropped down the other side. And again. And again.

And then the set had rolled by, and they were safely behind the break.

Steve and Dana sat up on their board and caught their breath.

Something was happening on the yacht.

Its sails were unfurled, and it was on the move.

Unguarded, Mickey and the doctor had left the saloon and retaken the boat!

The yacht sailed away from Steve and Dana.

"What about us?" Steve said. "We saved those guys."

Steve and Dana waved their arms wildly over their heads, but the boat was slowly receding.

"Those finks!" Steve said.

"Hey!" shouted Dana.

They screamed and waved.

The yacht started to turn.

It made a wide arc and was now coming right for them.

Steve and Dana let out happy cries and paddled toward the yacht.

It was picking up speed and coming right for them.

A shout rang out across the water. "Outside!"

Oh no.

"Outside!"

No, no, no.

"Outside!"

Another set was rolling in, and this one was breaking farther back than the last. Steve and Dana got on their stomachs and paddled.

"That boat needs to move!" Dana said. "It's going to capsize!"

There was no way the yacht could turn around in time. It was sailing in the wrong direction. As the boys were paddling east, the boat was coming west, rolling forward with the set, right toward the impact zone.

As Steve and Dana were sucked upward, the yacht plummeted by them, straight down the face of the wave. Its prow pointed downward.

Steve and Dana made it out over the back of the wave as the boat slammed into the ocean floor. When Steve and Dana looked back, the yacht's stern was sticking straight out of the water like a tombstone.

Steve checked the sea. It had been a rogue wave. The ocean was quiet.

"Look! They're alive!" Dana said.

Steve turned and saw two figures jump from the yacht into the water.

The yacht, almost completely vertical, creaked in the chop, and its boom swung to and fro.

"Well, now we're really stuck," Dana said.

CHAPTER L

A DARING PLAN

"NEW PLAN," said Steve. "We need to get over to that yacht."

"But—" Dana said, but Steve was already paddling.

Soon they were alongside the shipwreck. The back half of the yacht rose up above them. Its prow was deep underneath them—along with two freighters and hundreds of Lamborghinis.

Steve sat on the board and looked at his chum.

"Okay. What does an EPIRB look like?" he asked.

"Oh no," Dana said.

"Tell me," Steve said. The emergency beacon was still up in the stern of the ship, in the lifeboat. It was their only hope.

"It's yellow and white," Dana said. "It'll be in a box, strapped into the Zodiac."

"How does it work?" Steve said. "Fast."

"It'll look like a capsule. Flip the white cap off the top. There'll be a switch. You flip it on."

"That's it?"

"That's it. It sends out a satellite signal."

"Okay."

"How are you going to get up there?"

Steve looked up at the yacht. "The guardrails," he said. Now that the ship was on its side, the cables, crossed by supports, looked like a ladder—a very inconvenient ladder with rungs four feet apart.

"I'm coming with you," Dana said.

"No. You need to go get Mickey and Dr. Omond. They don't have wetsuits. Get them on the board."

Dana bit his lip. "Fine."

Steve hopped off the board and swam over to the *Boardwalker*.

CHAPTER LI

LADDER TO PERIL

THE GANGWAY rose straight up in front of Steve's face. He craned his neck upward and counted the rungs. Ten. Forty feet to the top. He'd better get started.

The first stanchion was just a few inches above the surface. Steve stepped onto it. It sagged under his weight, and he grabbed the next rung. It was right below his neck.

This wasn't going to be easy.

Steve contorted and stretched and pulled himself up.

He got his feet on that pole and reached up for the next rung.

That was one. This *really* wasn't going to be easy. The pole dug into the soles of his feet. Steve pulled. Two.

The boat was pitching and rolling. Steve's arms were burning.

Pull-ups had always been his least favorite part of the President's Physical Fitness Test. Steve typically maxed out at three. And while these weren't quite pull-ups, they were close.

Three, four.

The transverse cables Steve stood on were not meant to support a lot of weight. Each time he climbed up a rung, it gave a bit beneath him.

Five. The wind was blowing. Steve's hands were numb. He couldn't feel his feet, either, but he thought they might be bleeding. A clump of wet hair fell in Steve's eyes, and there was nothing he could do about it.

Six. Steve looked down. He was more than twenty feet up now. If he fell, he'd land in the water, which was sort of comforting, but he wasn't sure he could make it up again. And then they'd all drown ten miles off the coast of California. That was not comforting.

Seven.

Steve didn't know what made him look left, but when he did, he saw the boom swinging toward him.

He pressed himself against the deck. The boom missed him by inches. It swung back.

Steve hauled himself onto the eighth rung and grabbed the ninth.

The cable beneath his feet snapped. Steve dangled thirty-six feet above the sea.

CHAPTER LII

ABOARD THE WRECK

IT WAS ONE pull-up. Steve could do a pull-up.

But his arms were tired.

He flexed his biceps.

His knuckles bulged.

He rose a couple inches, then fell. Steve's feet were kicking at nothing.

Again. Again. He pulled himself upward.

The pole he was grabbing groaned.

He kept pulling.

He got his chin above the rung.

The yacht pitched. Steve thudded into the deck.

But the sway of the ship reduced the angle of

Steve's ascent. He closed his eyes and pulled as the *Boardwalker* moved. He got one knee onto the last stanchion, and then the other. In one desperate motion, Steve rose to his feet and slapped both hands onto the stern of the ship. He pulled himself up one last time. Steve Brixton was standing four stories above the Pacific on the back of a luxury yacht.

The Zodiac boat was on its side, strapped to a platform just in front of him. A few uneasy steps and he was there.

He ran his hands along the slippery rubber floor beneath the bench.

There was something plastic attached to the bottom of the boat. It was a box. Steve felt for a latch.

Saltines, water bottles, and flares came spilling down and caught in the lip of the Zodiac.

The moon was right overhead. Steve got on his hands and knees. He peered into the lifeboat.

There. Something white and yellow, the size of Steve's forearm. He grabbed it.

The EPIRB looked a little like an ice cream cone with an antenna coming out the top.

Steve popped off the beacon's white cap.

The yacht continued to sway beneath him. To steady himself, he grabbed the Zodiac with his left hand. He looked out at the water.

Steve teetered above the Pacific.

Another wave was rolling in. It was a black-green monster with a foaming white lip.

Steve examined the device. There was a big red switch with black letters: ON.

The wave drew itself up as it steamed forward. It was as tall as Steve was high. And it was coming right for him.

Steve had a choice: jump in the water and try to swim through a vertical wall of water, or take his chances here on the *Boardwalker*.

The wave roared.

Steve took a deep breath.

He flipped the switch on the beacon and jumped off the yacht, right into the cresting colossus before him.

CHAPTER LIII

BACK ASHORE

THE COAST GUARD chopper touched down on the beach so Steve and Dana could watch the Berserkers come in on the cutters.

Steve looked down in the dark and saw flashing lights of police cruisers and unmarked cars. News vans with satellite antennas poking up from their roofs like bean shoots were parked along the highway. There were a lot of people on the beach.

The helicopter blew sand all around as it landed. The pilot cut the motor. A crowd swarmed the chopper's passengers as they were helped onto the ground. A reporter shoved a microphone in Dr.

Omond's face. Steve and Dana were surrounded by Carol Brixton, the Villalons, Rick, and Chief Clumber.

Steve leaned toward the chief. "It was the Berserkers," he said. "You should have arrested them when I told you to."

Steve's mom drew him into a tight hug.

Rick had his hand on Mickey's shoulder. "Yeah, even for an experienced waterman, giant waves can be scary. I remember this one time, it must have been double overhead and there was this monster riptide. I was the only one . . ." Steve noticed that Rick's blond mustache was coffee stained.

Then Steve and Dana were shoved in front of the chopper, and a reporter for the *Outlook* snapped their photograph. Steve realized after the flash went off that he was still wearing his life vest, which was a little too tight and came up right under his chin. He hadn't even been given the vest until he was out of the water, and now here he was wearing it on dry land in a picture for the papers. He looked at Dana. His chum had taken his off.

Chief Clumber let Steve and Dana sit in the back of his squad car to avoid the hubbub. They wrapped themselves in itchy green blankets and drank hot chocolate.

"Well, that takes care of two cases," Dana said.

"But I guess we may never solve the Case of the Missing Gym Shorts."

Steve took a long sip and wiped some whipped cream off his nose. "Oh, I solved that one," Steve said. "Brody was taking his own gym shorts."

"What?" said Dana. "Why would you think that?"

"They were last stolen on Tuesday, right? Monday was a holiday, and Mr. Owens was washing Brody's P.E. clothes over the weekend. Brody has P.E. first period, so there's no way they could have been taken from his locker. They should have been in his backpack."

"But why would he steal his own shorts?"

"Probably because he didn't want to run the mile."

"Huh?"

"That roster you stole from Coach P., the one with everybody's mile times on it? It had every last name but Owens. Brody Owens has never run the mile. Probably because he doesn't want to get all sweaty."

"Then why did Brody hire you?"

"Well, he *tried* to hire me to get his dad off his case. He probably figured I wouldn't solve it. Lots of people hire detectives so they'll look innocent. They always think they're smarter than the sleuths."

"So nobody stole any gym shorts."

"Nope."

"And nobody broke into a locked locker."

"Right."

"Huh."

"I know."

"Well, that's disappointing."

Steve took another sip. "I know. Sometimes the sleuthing is more exciting than the solving."

Dana murmured something and drank his hot chocolate.

Steve did feel pretty good about sending the Berserkers to jail, though. He hoped that when the judge put them in the slammer for piracy, smuggling, and kidnapping, he would remember to add some time for breaking Danimal's surfboard. Steve wondered whether the knowledge that these guys were getting locked up would make Danimal feel a little better about losing his board. He remembered his client's face when he'd seen those broken pieces, and he doubted it.

Soon there was a commotion on the beach, as two Coast Guard cutters docked at a jetty. Steve and Dana got out of Clumber's cruiser to watch the eight Berserkers walk, in cuffs, up the pier. Tremblay scowled. The chimp was without his mask. Tremor wasn't wearing his hat.

A man in a suit led Tremor to a black sedan. "Hey, Trem!" Steve said.

The Berserker looked up. "What, kook?"

"I figured out the difference between people like you and people like me."

Steve paused for effect.

"People like me put people like you in jail."

Tremor smirked. The man in the suit made sure the Berserker hit his head on the roof when he forced him into the back of the car.

As the sun came up, Steve and Dana walked over to their parents. Steve yawned. It was time to get home. Tomorrow he'd get a letter from Claire Marriner. Next week he would receive *A Message from a Maniac.*